ISBN: 978-0-9885822-6-2
Published by Samantha Sabian and Arianthem Press
THE RIVAL'S CONCORD Vol 4 CHRONICLES OF ARIANTHEM, 2014. FIRST PRINTING.
Office of Publication: Los Angeles, California

What did you think of this book? We love to hear from our readers.
Please email us at: samantha@arianthem.com.

THE RIVAL'S CONCORD
THE CHRONICLES OF ARIANTHEM IV

by Samantha Sabian

SECOND CHRONICLES

THE DRAGON'S NIGHT
2nd CHRONICLES OF ARIANTHEM I (Book 9)
(ISBN: 978-1-943728-06-0)

THE SCINTERIAN'S DREAM
2ND CHRONICLES OF ARIANTHEM II (Book 10)
(ISBN: 978-1-943728-08-4)

THE RISE OF THE SINISTER
2ND CHRONICLES OF ARIANTHEM III (Book 11)
(ISBN: 978-1-943728-14-5)

visit us on the web at

www.arianthem.com

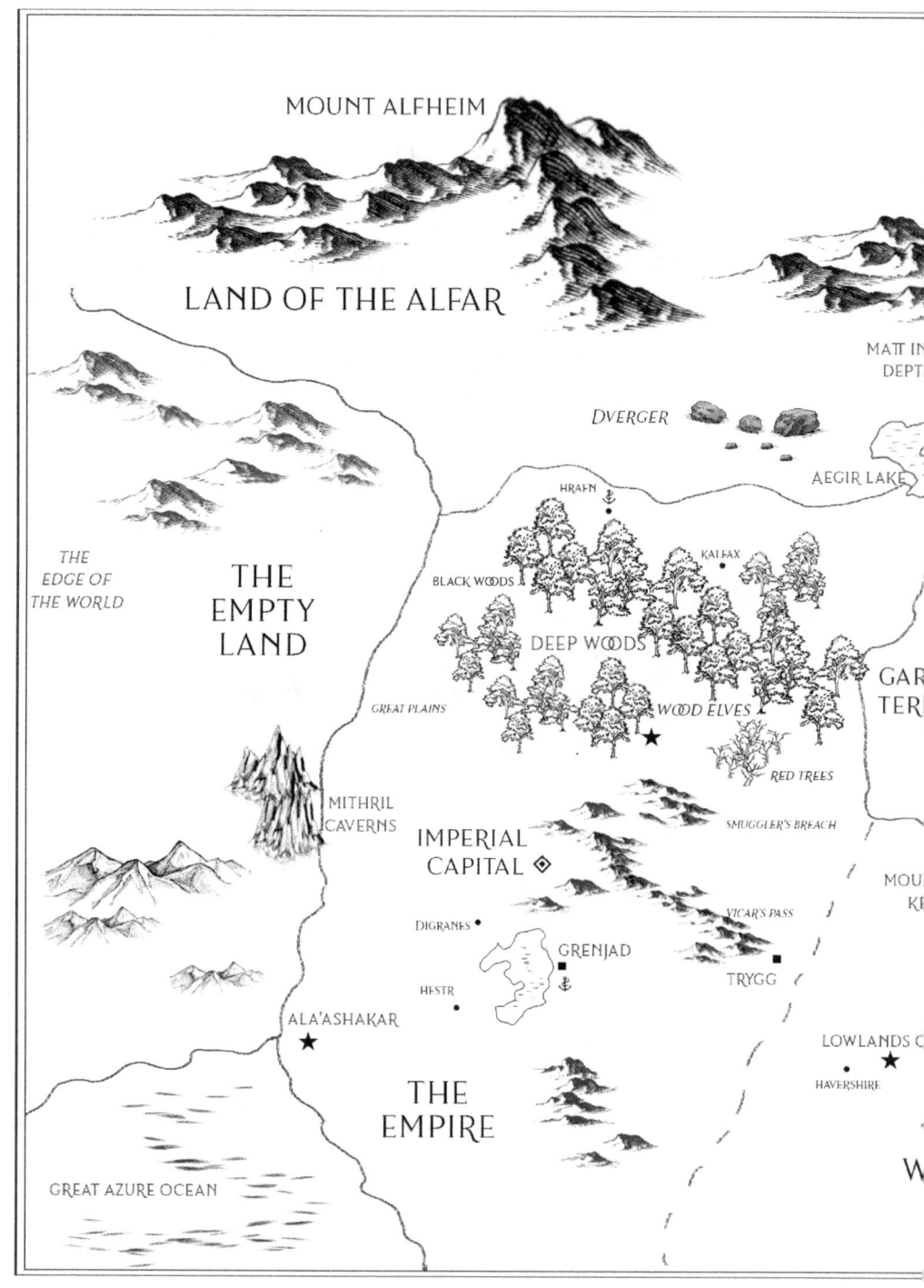

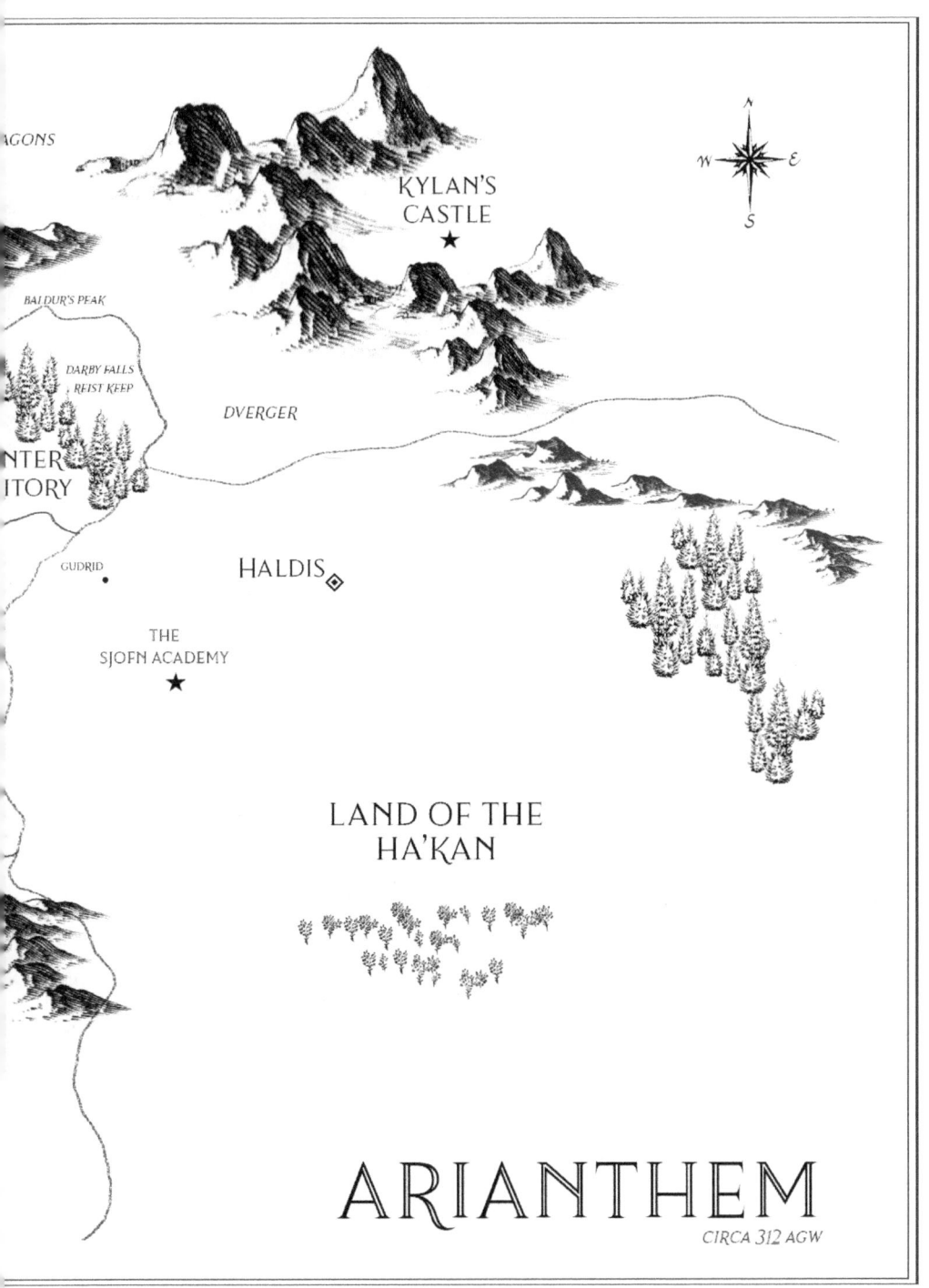

AGONS

KYLAN'S
CASTLE
★

BALDUR'S PEAK

DARBY FALLS
REIST KEEP

DVERGER

NTER
ITORY

GUDRID

HALDIS ◈

THE
SJOFN ACADEMY
★

LAND OF THE
HA'KAN

ARIANTHEM

CIRCA 312 AGW

Chapter 1

Skye awoke to the loveliest, filmy curtains over her bed. She stared up at the iridescent color, enjoying the little rainbows that formed as the sheer cloth moved in the gentle breeze. She was drowsy and comfortable and hadn't the slightest idea where she was. She looked down at the naked woman in her arms and smiled. She was not in her own bed, which was part of her mild disorientation. She was in Lifa's bed in her chambers in the Ministry building.

Lifa stirred, then stretched, which pressed her full breasts up against Skye's lean torso much to Skye's enjoyment. She reached down and caressed Lifa's hip, which caused Lifa to sigh with pleasure in her half-sleep and press closer to her. Skye buried her head in Lifa's auburn hair, which elicited another murmur of pleasure and brought Lifa fully from her sleep. She looked up, her brown eyes full of love and laughter. Lifa turned to the open window where the gentle breeze was coming from, noting that the sun was already halfway to its peak.

"You're keeping me from my duties," Lifa chastised, "they'll accuse us of being exclusive if you keep this up."

Skye laughed. Lifa was a Priestess of the Ha'kan, an all-female race that eschewed monogamy. Sexual activity was so woven into the fabric of their society that the third branch of their culture, the Ministry, was devoted entirely to the sexual health of their people. Relationships, whether casual or professional, were augmented by this sexual bonding, and as a result, ability in the bedroom was as important as any other skill or expertise. And Lifa was a very special Priestess, one who despite her young age had already been added to the staff of the Queen's High Priestess, Astrid. It was widely recognized that Lifa would succeed Astrid when Queen Halla relinquished the throne to her daughter, Dallan.

"I doubt any would accuse either of us of that offense," Skye said, her eyes soft. "I just missed you."

Lifa rolled over on top of her. "I missed you, too. And my Priestesses miss you as well. You were hardly healed when you took off on your little jaunt. And although Ama takes her duties seriously and doesn't play favorites, I feel she's missed you particularly."

"Ah," Skye said, beaming. Although she was Tavinter and one of the few non-Ha'kan welcomed into their society, she eagerly embraced their open ways. The thought of Ama, the short, voluptuous little Priestess who was part of Lifa's inner circle filled Skye with warmth. "I'll see her tonight, then." She stopped, realizing she was being presumptuous. "If that works into her schedule and you approve, of course."

Lifa inwardly smiled. Scheduling was always done by the Priestesses, not by the women they serviced. The Ministry assigned trysts based upon perceived needs and compatibility, as well as any identified deficiencies in skill or training. But Skye had no deficiencies and was compatible with everyone, for she was known as a gentle but passionate lover, and she was a favorite of the Priestesses despite their vows not to play favorites.

"I have a feeling her schedule will be open," Lifa said, "and I approve as much for her well-being as yours."

"Good, that'll give me something to look forward to. I have a very busy day." She rose and pulled on her clothes beneath Lifa's appreciative gaze. "If you don't stop looking at me like that," Skye said, buttoning her shirt, "I'll climb right back in that bed with you."

"That's not the way to discourage me," Lifa said, "now get out of my chambers before I keep you here the rest of the day."

Skye stumbled out into the hallway, still adjusting her clothing, and nearly ran right into Astrid. She blushed crimson under the elegant woman's assessment.

"High Priestess," Skye mumbled in greeting.

"Getting a late start on the day, are we?" Astrid said.

"Um, yes, apparently so," Skye said, realizing how late it was. "If you'll excuse me," she said with a respectful bow, then practically ran down the hallway to escape the scrutiny of the High Priestess. Astrid watched the girl flee with amusement, although technically she wasn't a girl any longer. Skye had turned from a beautiful girl into a gorgeous young woman. She was still younger than her cohort because she had come to the Sjöfn Academy young and been adopted by Dallan's inner circle, who were several years older and in their final year at the time. Had Skye finished the Academy, she would have graduated only last year.

Astrid knocked lightly on the half-open door to Lifa's chambers, then pushed her way inside. Lifa smiled warmly at the High Priestess, demonstrating none of Skye's bashfulness. The last few years she had spent many a night in Astrid's bed, learning some of the more esoteric techniques a High Priestess might need. Bashfulness was rare in the Ha'kan and although endearing in Skye, would be a detriment in a Priestess.

"Good morning, High Priestess."

"Good morning, Lifa," Astrid said, admiring the young woman's curves as she pulled on her robe. "And how are you today?"

"I'm wonderful, Astrid. Thank you."

"And how is Skye?" Astrid asked.

"I think she's still making up for lost time," Lifa said, and the faintest trace of a cloud crossed the perennial sun of her disposition. Skye had been taken from them through a series of tragic events. When she was finally returned, it was only briefly because she was then taken again, this time by a sorceress who tortured and nearly killed her. Skye spent months recovering from her illness, and when at last she was well, had disappeared for a few weeks on some recent mysterious expedition. Lifa had made her promise she would not go anywhere for a while.

"Yes, I imagine so," Astrid said. Although she thought of Skye as the little beauty who had enamored them all at the Academy, she had to remind herself that the girl was also the leader of the Tavinter, one who had successfully waged a guerilla war for years against the Ha'kan, an especially impressive feat considering the Ha'kan military rivaled that of the empire. Still, the girl was young, and if she was to occupy the high place in Ha'kan society that had been offered her, then Astrid was responsible for her sexual development and by extension, so was Lifa.

"Is Skye aware that although sex is always pleasurable, it's not always strictly for pleasure?"

"I believe she understands the idea in concept." A memory brought a twinkle to Lifa's eye. "She did provide pleasure for half her class in a single night at the Academy, and that seemed out of obligation."

"Ah, that's right," Astrid said, smiling at the reminder. That incident had been the topic of conversation even amongst the royal staff. "Good. There's a contingent coming from the western holds. There will be many meetings, formal dinners, entertainment, the like, and someone may take an interest in her."

"I have no doubt of that," Lifa said, "and although Skye is still shy, I think she'll respond appropriately."

"Good. There's a second matter. I know that Skye enjoys your company and spends a great deal of time with Dallan and Rika as well as the Priestesses."

"Yes, and Kara as well," Lifa said.

"How could I forget Kara?" Astrid said wryly. "But has Skye been with any older women?"

"We're all older than Skye, but I think I know what you mean, and the answer is no."

"Hmm," Astrid said, "I wish her to experience that sometime soon."

"Are you thinking of taking her to your bed?" Lifa asked curiously.

"I've had that thought from the day she showed up at the Academy," Astrid admitted without hesitation, "even prior to her Age of Consent. But that's not my motivation. From my understanding, she's an excellent lover and I want that progress to continue."

"Of course, High Priestess, I'll discuss it with her. Do you have any suggestions?"

Astrid waved her hand. "No, no. You can decide that. I'm sure your judgment will prove sound as always."

"Thank you," Lifa said, nodding as Astrid stood. The High Priestess started towards the door, then paused in the entryway. Lifa loved her elegant, sultry manner and hoped one day she could emulate it.

"Don't mistake me. I would take Skye to my bed tonight. I just fear she would run in terror at the thought because she still can't look me in the eye without blushing."

"The Tavinter do run like the wind," Lifa said, laughter in her eyes, "but I have a feeling you would catch her, High Priestess."

Skye took two wrong turns, then stood baffled in the center of the hallway. She was still getting used to living in the royal palace. Dallan had insisted she maintain quarters here as was appropriate for her staff, and Skye's suite sat between Dallan's and Kara's and across the circular forum from Rika's, and Lifa's. Unfortunately, she didn't know where any of those were right now and was afraid she would wander into the housing of the Queen's staff which was opposite Dallan's. She had done that once before, mistaking the Queen's forum for Dallan's, and the smoldering gaze of the High Priestess and the graceful sensuality of Queen Halla herself had haunted Skye's dreams for a week.

The guards looked at Skye and the one nearest her shook her head, chuckling. That lovely little Tavinter did this about once a day. She pointed down the hallway in the right direction.

"Thank you," Skye mumbled, "this place is just so big." She would not get lost in a thousand square miles of forest, but she could not navigate the palace.

Skye found her room and pushed through the double doors with relief. Her chambers were huge and luxurious, and she was overwhelmed every time she walked into them. There was an enormous bed in the sleeping area, but it might as well have been a cot because Skye rarely slept there. Although she changed clothing and bathed in her chambers, more often than not she slept in one of the other suites.

She peered out her window into the courtyard. She had thought the Sjöfn Academy was a beautiful place, but the Ha'kan Royal Palace was a wonder to behold. The capital itself was impressive, with exquisite architecture, cobblestone streets, marbled walkways, areas of greenery filled with flowers and statuary, and the Palace was the jewel of the city. It sat high on the hill and was built in a square, each side dedicated to one of the three major branches of Ha'kan society, the Priestess caste, the Warrior caste, and the Scholar caste, with the fourth side occupied by the Ha'kan royal family and staff. Much like the Academy, there was an outdoor area set aside for training. An elaborate garden bordered the Ministry Building where the majority of the Priestesses lived, a garden which extended into a more private area that was adjacent to the quarters of the royal family and accessible from Skye's room and the rooms of all the royal staff. Skye had not ventured out to the private garden just yet, but Dallan had given her a wicked grin and told her she would give her a personal tour very soon.

Skye bathed and then pulled on her lightweight training armor. The leather straps gleamed and the subtle eagle outline on the chest gave her a little thrill. This armor was Tavinter but had been slightly altered when the Tavinter had agreed to act as a scouting regiment for the Ha'kan army. The armor had always been functional, but the Ha'kan added beauty to everything, and their stylish touch was evident.

The forum was empty when she left her room, and Skye hoped she had not kept Dallan and Rika waiting too long on the training field. She passed Kara's room and wondered if the lithesome scholar was in there. Kara kept the oddest hours and had chambers in the Scholar's wing as well, much like Lifa who often slept at the Ministry as part of her duties. Because of that, Skye also slept in the Scholar's wing on occasion, and spent half her time sleeping at the Ministry, either in the arms of Lifa or one of the Priestesses. Such a practice might have been disorienting for some, but Skye was from a nomadic people and it felt quite natural. Additionally, she had slept in her own bed at the Academy on few occasions and Dallan had commented that Skye didn't really need one.

Skye found her way out much easier than her way in and trotted down the marble steps leading from the palace. She nodded to those she passed, and they returned the cordial greeting. Skye was not quite certain how the majority of the Ha'kan felt about her. Through no fault of her own or that of her people, she had waged war against them for three years. Although it was later found that neither side had committed the atrocities the other believed, Skye wondered if any held a grudge against her. She knew there were some among the Tavinter who still held hard feelings for the Ha'kan, especially those who had lost someone in the war. But the majority understood the deception had been perpetrated by the Garmlain, and the fact that the Ha'kan had turned about and utterly destroyed the Garmlain soothed the hearts of many.

The mild unease these thoughts caused increased when she walked onto the training field. She had spent many hours in swordplay and archery at the Academy, but this was the first time she had trained with the Ha'kan troops since her return. She felt the weight of hundreds of eyes upon her, a weight that seemed to grow heavier when she did not see Dallan or Rika. She scuffed her boot in the dirt. She was supposed to be in charge of the new regiment of Tavinter scouts, a very high-ranking position within the Ha'kan military, but right now she felt like it was her first day at the Academy all over again.

The Ha'kan warriors examined the newcomer with interest. They had heard tales of this one's exploits at the Academy, and her ghostly presence in the Tavinter forests during the war was legendary. Still, it was hard to square that image of her with the slender figure who stood before them. Skye was tall for a Tavinter, but that meant she was not even of average height for a Ha'kan. Also, she was far younger than any had imagined. Her discomfort and uncertainty were obvious.

"Well, she's a gorgeous little thing, I'll give you that," one soldier whispered. "But she looks more like a priestess than a warrior."

"By the gods, can you imagine that one in your bed?" another soldier whispered back. "I have a sword I'd like to show her how to use."

One of the Royal Guard, a member of far higher rank than the two whispering behind her, overheard the remarks. She had been assigned to Queen Halla's contingent at the Academy and had ridden with the Princess's regiment during the war. As a member of the Royal Guard, she was older and far more experienced than the two behind her, and she had seen Skye in action firsthand.

"You'd be wise not to judge her by her appearance," she said over her shoulder, "and give her the respect her position deserves. Besides," she said, turning to look at them. "She'll take that 'sword' and break it over your head."

"Yes, commander," the two responded in unison, embarrassed they had been overheard. Still, as their eyes returned to the tentative figure in front of them, that hardly seemed likely.

Skye was relieved to see Dallan and Rika approaching on horseback. They flew in at breakneck speed and both looked splendid in their gleaming armor, Rika's emblazoned with garlands indicating her rank and Dallan's slightly modified to indicate her royal status. They were both grinning at their impromptu race, one that Dallan just barely won. Rika calmed her rearing horse, and both dismounted. Their excitement and joy were infectious and all the Ha'kan felt it: this was their beloved Princess and her capable right hand. Both had won the hearts of their people by exemplary leadership and bravery in battle despite their youth. Although Skye was happy to see them, their impressive appearance magnified her current feeling of inadequacy.

The imagined inadequacy was nowhere in Dallan's sight as she gazed at Skye. She could only marvel at how good Skye looked in that scout armor, which made her want to pull Skye into the nearby armory and take it off of her. Rika, too, examined her with admiration.

"Finally able to drag yourself from Lifa's bed?" Rika said, and Skye frowned at her.

Dallan nudged Rika. "Got bumped from Lifa's schedule, did you?"

"Can you believe it?" Rika said with mock indignation. "Training needs, she said."

A retort was on Skye's lips, but this caught her attention. "Training needs," she said, concerned, "does Lifa think me deficient?"

This caused both Rika and Dallan to burst into laughter. "Oh yes," Rika said, "I think half the Priestess caste wishes to assist you in remedial training."

It seemed they were teasing her, but Skye wasn't entirely certain. "Well, I'm sorry if I bumped you from Lifa's schedule."

"'Tis no matter," Rika said, "I've been rescheduled for this evening. And you," she said with a gleam in her eye, "will pay me back."

Skye frowned again. That generally meant that within a day or two she would be face down somewhere with Rika mounting her from behind. The thought was as arousing as it was distracting.

"Come, you two, we have to focus," Dallan said, turning to address the troops. "We'll warm up with the Progression," she said loudly, "so pair off and begin."

The troops all found a partner, decided who would attack and who would defend, and began the elaborate exercise. The Progression was a choreographed series of strikes and parries designed to teach basic to advanced skills. It was taught at the Academy and then used for on-going training. Dallan and Rika watched for a moment, then Rika turned to Dallan and drew her sword.

"Wait, wait," she said, and Skye braced herself at Rika's mocking tone, "who am I?"

Rika held the sword at an awkward angle and Dallan knew immediately what she was talking about. Dallan drew her own sword and knocked the one from Rika's hand while Rika made herself look as incompetent as possible. They both burst into laughter as Skye looked at them blackly. They were making fun of her. When she had been a new student at the Academy, she had hidden her considerable skill by performing as poorly as possible, an attempt to blend in that had backfired. She had fooled everyone except Dallan, who watched her attempt the Progression but one time and called her bluff, forcing Skye to fight her. The ensuing swordplay had been epic.

"Do you even remember the Progression?" Dallan asked, swinging her sword about playfully.

Skye drew her own sword, and the feel of the hilt in her hand soothed her. Dallan felt a thrill of anticipation because the change in Skye's demeanor was instant. Whereas most became more agitated and aggressive with a weapon in their hand, Skye was the opposite. She became calm and composed, transitioning from a little woman-child to one of the most dangerous individuals Dallan had ever met. Dallan would have loved Skye for her beauty and skill in bed, but she adored her for her skill in battle.

"I remember it," Skye said, "would you like to test me?"

Rika observed the impending challenge and could not resist playing instigator.

"I think a wager is in order," Rika suggested.

"I think that's a very good idea," Dallan said, swinging her sword arm to loosen up, "we'll wager for earth or sky."

Skye swung her own sword about. "Just so I'm clear, if I win, I get to be sky?"

"You get to be whatever you want," Dallan said nonchalantly. "Tomorrow night. In the garden."

"In the garden?" Skye said, shocked, for they were discussing who would get to be in the dominant position for sex.

"Yes," Dallan said carelessly, "in the garden. It can be quite private there. Or not, depending on your wishes."

Skye's cheeks reddened. "The privacy is not part of the wager, is it?"

"Ah," Rika said knowingly. "I think I've identified a training need. I'll have to tell Lifa."

"You will not!" Skye exclaimed, although she knew Rika would at the first opportunity.

"Are we going to do this or not?" Dallan asked, now that she was certain Skye was completely distracted. She took her position, and Skye, after throwing a dark look in Rika's direction, took the counter position. Rika noted they looked more like a graceful pair of dancers than two about to engage in a brutal fight.

Dallan initiated and took the first swing at Skye who, despite the speed and force of the blow, parried it without effort. Dallan struck twice, Skye parried, Dallan struck thrice, Skye parried, and so the Progression began. And it did indeed look like a dance as the two began moving far earlier than the Progression called for. And they were completing it with such speed they had already surpassed those who had begun far earlier.

"Do you want to stop at fifty?" Dallan said, only slightly out of breath.

"Are you tired?" Skye said, not out of breath at all.

"One hundred it is," Dallan said, and swung her sword with blinding speed. Rika crossed her arms over her chest. These two were not even breathing hard whereas many of the soldiers who were finishing were covered in sweat and gasping for air. The Progression was brutally difficult so that was expected, but even so, this pair provided a great example for conditioning.

As the two continued their fierce contest, more and more of the soldiers finished and began to gather around. It took the combatants longer to reach the hundredth strike for each round, a single strike was added, but everything was repeated. By this time, both Skye and Dallan were showing signs of exertion, although still less than expected. After the one hundredth strike, the Progression moved to free work, which could sometimes be dangerous as the participants were so fatigued, control could become an issue. Still, the Ha'kan Princess and the Tavinter sparred full force without pulling their strikes in any way. Both were perfectly in control despite the length of their contest.

Which is why Rika was greatly surprised when Dallan dropped her guard. It was so dramatic an error that Rika flinched because Skye was coming in full force, and Dallan did not appear to be responding in time, or even responding at all. At the last second, with monumental effort, Skye stopped her blow which would have otherwise killed Dallan. The effort required was so great, Skye staggered off balance, dug her sword into the earth, then flipped herself to dissipate her momentum. She lay on her back looking up at the clouds, her chest heaving from exertion.

Rika looked to Dallan with disapproval and admiration. Disapproval for dropping her guard, but admiration for the devious tactic. "That was mean," she said, and Dallan just grinned. Dallan walked over to Skye, sticking her own sword into the earth.

"I guess this means I win the wager."

Skye looked up at her. "That wasn't fair."

Dallan helped her to her feet, wanting to kiss her right there and almost did. "You're right. It wasn't. But I'll collect my bet nonetheless."

Rika turned to the watching crowd. "Now that's the example I want you to follow," she said, drawing her own sword to begin the training in earnest. "Except for that last part," she said, turning to frown at Dallan but not Skye. Dallan just grinned wickedly.

"What just happened?"

The soldier who had earlier whispered about conquering Skye in bed had watched the contest in astonishment. She had completely reevaluated her opinion of the Tavinter, but the end of the fight had left her puzzled. The Royal Guard who had chastised her smiled. Dallan was not only brilliant at swordplay, she was wise beyond her years, for she had communicated something far clearer through action than words.

"The Princess lowered her guard on purpose."

"Why would she do that?"

"Because she cheated," the guard said.

"How did she cheat?" the soldier asked, still puzzled.

"She knew that Skye wouldn't strike her down." The Royal Guard turned to all the soldiers who were listening to the conversation to make certain Dallan's message was delivered.

"The Princess trusts that Tavinter with her life."

Skye trained for hours with the soldiers, and her unease dissipated.

As the drills continued, she found herself more and more paired with the Royal Guard who sought her out because of her skill. All Ha'kan warriors were dangerous in battle, but the Guard were the elite, and this Tavinter's skill was a whetstone for their swords. Rika observed this with great pleasure because she was responsible for the readiness of her regiment, and until Senta returned, she was responsible for the Guard as well. She was also pleased with Skye's near-instantaneous integration back into the Ha'kan forces. She knew that her influence and even more so, Dallan's, would carry great weight. But it appeared that influence was hardly needed.

Rika herself engaged Skye many times, and theirs was always an interesting battle. Dallan was larger than Skye, but their fighting styles were similar. Rika was much larger than Skye, not only in height but in pure physical size. Skye gave a textbook lesson on how to bedevil a much larger foe as she danced about, dodging Rika's blows, never allowing one to fall with full force. Rika was not slow, she was dangerously fast for her size, but even so, she was no match for Skye's speed and dexterity, and Skye was very good at using Rika's weight and momentum against her. It was unlikely Skye could defeat Rika, but it was just as unlikely that Rika would defeat Skye.

"You see, this is why I pin you down," Rika said, blocking Skye's thrust with her shield.

"Oh, so that's your excuse," Skye said, swinging again.

Rika blocked the blow, this one that was at her head. "Actually, I just like you thrashing around beneath me."

"I do not thrash," Skye said, "and why is it you put me face-down? Don't you like to look at me?"

Skye's sword struck with such force on Rika's shield, the sound drew the attention of those around them. Rika grinned.

"I love to look at your face. Why do think I put you on your hands and knees in front of a mirror?"

"Damn you!" Skye said, striking with even greater force and attracting more attention. But Rika's teasing was not making Skye angry. If anything, it was exciting her, and Skye was hitting harder so she could maintain her concentration.

Rika realized they were attracting too much attention. "Stop," she said, laughing. She moved closer to Skye to end their battle. "Stop, or I'll take you to the ground right here and we'll work on your 'privacy' issue."

Skye lowered her sword. "You would, too, wouldn't you?"

"With complete and utter abandon," Rika said. "Now I think we're done, or I'll have nothing left for Lifa."

"Don't blame your shortcomings on me," Skye said mischievously, then darted from Rika's attempted grab.

"You're going to pay for that," Rika called after her as Skye ran from the field, laughing. "I'll just add it to your debt."

Chapter 2

Dallan's inner circle had fallen back into the habit of meeting in Lifa's chambers at fourth bell. They had done it regularly at the Academy and the tradition had waned during the war. But when Skye returned, they fell back into the comfortable routine as if it had never stopped. Lifa more often than not stayed at the Ministry building and the Ha'kan population was grateful, for it allowed them far more access to the Princess and her staff, even if it was from a distance and only in passing. It was not that Queen Halla was inaccessible, for she was considered quite approachable if need be. It was simply that the Princess was less formal than her regal mother, a role that Halla had played when her mother had been on the throne.

Dallan was grateful for the ritual because it allowed her to keep her staff close and bonded with little effort. Plus, it was incredibly enjoyable and something they all looked forward to each day. She was already lying on Lifa's couch with her head in Lifa's lap when Rika walked in and sprawled onto the couch as well. Lifa's chambers were much like they were at the Academy, with the cushy, semi-circular sitting area, but the suite was larger and more luxurious. There were several bedrooms off the main room, each separated by a series of sheer veils. Rika kissed Ama, who although always lively, was in a particularly good mood, which Rika commented upon.

"Ama has an appointment with Skye," Lifa explained.

"Say no more," Rika said. "Although she might be a little tired as the entire Ha'kan army tried to wear her down without success. And Dallan tried to kill her."

The future High Priestess ran her fingers through Dallan's hair. "And what did you do to our little Tavinter?"

"I left myself wide open and I think she pulled every muscle in her body trying to stop her attack. She actually flipped herself to stop the blow."

The fingers ran through the hair again and Lifa leaned down to kiss Dallan's forehead. "You're cruel," she said.

Skye strolled in and Ama was pleased to see she did not look the least bit tired. She stopped to give Lifa a kiss which Lifa passionately returned. Dallan took that opportunity to snatch her by the collar and playfully pull her down on top of her, causing Lifa to laugh.

"Are you mad at me?" Dallan asked.

"Of course, I am, you idiot. I could have killed you."

"Idiot?" Dallan said teasingly, "I hardly think that's how you should address royalty." Dallan was holding her tightly, enjoying the lithe form on top of her while she got to stare into those lovely hazel eyes.

"You're a royal pain in my backside," Skye said.

"No, that's Kara's job," Dallan said, eliciting laughter from everyone. Kara was known for unconventional sexual exploration. "You still lost the wager."

"What wager is that?" Lifa asked.

"Earth or sky," Skye said darkly, "and of course I'm earth once more."

Dallan released her and Skye rolled off onto her feet.

"Come here, little one," Ama said soothingly. The endearment always amused Skye because Ama was one of the few Ha'kan that Skye actually dwarfed, especially now that she was fully grown. But Skye had once challenged Ama regarding the title and Ama had simply thrust her ample breasts in Skye's face, forcing Skye to agree that Ama was much larger than she was. She had not argued since. Skye settled in next to Ama, taking comfort as the voluptuous little Priestess pulled her down so that her head was in her lap. Skye liked this position because her cheek was pressed against those wonderful breasts.

"You may be earth or sky with me anytime," Ama said, stroking her hair, "and if they haven't experienced you on top, they don't know what they're missing."

"I can attest to that," Lifa said with emphasis.

Skye relaxed, feeling mildly redeemed, but then Lifa continued.

"That brings up another matter, however. Now that you're healthy again, I'm responsible for your development, and there's something I want you to think about."

Skye sat upright and looked accusingly as Rika. "You already told her?"

Rika had her hands behind her head as she leaned back, her long legs out in front of her. "No, I didn't say anything. But now that you've told on yourself, perhaps we should discuss that."

Skye sank back into Ama's lap in exasperation. Rika took more enjoyment from the confession than she would have from divulging the information herself. Dallan also immediately chimed in.

"Yes, Lifa, that's right. Skye expressed horror over having sex in the garden because of 'privacy' issues."

"I wasn't horrified," Skye said, sounding far more defensive than she wished, "I just, I was just—,"

"I see," Lifa said thoughtfully. She was delighted by Skye's discomfiture; it was so charming. "Exhibitionism does take some getting used to, meaning it would require some practice and probably repeated exposure." The pun also delighted her. "And really, we could all enjoy that."

"Ama, why don't you just strip her, and we'll start now?" Rika suggested.

"No," Skye said, trying to pull herself upright. But Ama caught her.

"Shh," she said, the priestess in her taking over. "At your own pace and in your own time," she counseled.

"That's right," Lifa said, gentling her teasing, "And only if you want to. You know I want you to try everything so that you'll know what you like."

Skye relaxed once more. Of course, she knew that.

Skye's reaction puzzled Dallan a little. Skye was normally open about all things sexual and although occasionally reserved, she could be quite adventurous. And Dallan knew that Skye had been with multiple partners at one time because she and Lifa had slept with Skye, and she and Rika often took her together, two combinations of sexual partners that most could not even handle. And Skye often 'entertained' more than a single Priestess at a time. Dallan wondered if perhaps it was the Tavinter instinct to remain unseen, to blend into the forest that was at play here, rather than anything to do with intercourse. If that was the case, she thought, grinning to herself, then overcoming that instinct could lead to some explosive sex.

"You're evil," Lifa whispered to her, reading her expression. She did, however, need to return to her original conversation.

"Actually, Skye, I had something else in mind. Have you been with any older women?"

This brought smiles all around, and now Skye was more curious than apprehensive. "You're all older than me," she said. "I don't think I've been with anyone younger than myself."

"No," Lifa said, "that's not what I'm talking about. We're all older than you, but only by a few years. I'm talking about someone significantly older. At least a decade, preferably two."

"No," Skye said with a little confusion, "I haven't. It seems that most Ha'kan stay within their age group by a few years."

"There's a reason for that," Lifa said, "Ha'kan women don't reach their sexual peak until their fourth, even fifth decade. And then they stay at that peak for a very long time."

Skye thought of the Queen and Astrid, her sultry, elegant High Priestess, then stared around the circle at her companions. "You're all going to get worse?" she said in disbelief.

"I prefer to think of it as getting better," Rika said with satisfaction, "but yes, we'll all get much, much worse."

Lifa tried to stay on track. "The older Ha'kan women stay with those in their age group because frankly, most of the younger women cannot," she sought a delicate way to say it, "keep up."

"By the gods," Skye murmured.

"But it's important for a younger woman to experience that at least once."

Skye looked askance at Lifa. "Have you been with any older woman?"

"Of course," Lifa said, "I've shared Astrid's bed many times."

"By the gods!" Skye sputtered again.

"It's required of my position," Lifa said. "There are many things she must teach me."

Skye could not even picture that, as much as she wanted to. She turned her head to Dallan.

"And have you slept with Astrid?"

"Oh no," Dallan said, "Astrid is too close to my mother, and too maternal towards me. And although that dynamic can be enjoyable—," as if to emphasize that fact, Ama pressed her breast to Skye's cheek and she fully understood, "I don't think that pairing would occur."

Skye had wondered about that. Ha'kan did not require a partner for reproduction, and pregnancy was entirely independent of sex. Clearly women did not engage in sexual relationships within their own bloodline, but outside of that, things got very vague as to what was acceptable. Skye thought she was beginning to understand, but Dallan's next words destroyed that idea.

"No, I slept with Lifa's mother."

"What?" Skye said in astonishment.

"I slept with Lifa's mother, too," Rika said. "It was extraordinary. It took me almost a week to recover."

Skye looked from one to the other, then to Lifa who appeared nothing more than pleased and proud. Skye realized she might not ever completely understand the Ha'kan.

"Well, all right then," Skye said, laying her head back down and staring up at the ceiling.

Lifa recognized that Skye was overwhelmed and would not push her further. "Just think about it, Skye. You know I have only your best interest at heart."

"I know," Skye said, still staring at the ceiling. Ama stroked her hair.

"Would you like to begin our appointment early?" she said.

"I think I'd like that very much," Skye said numbly, and Ama led her by the hand from the room.

"That poor thing," Lifa murmured.

"That poor thing?" Rika said, "Would that I had her problems. Sexual partners without end. Complete access to the Princess of the Ha'kan, the future High Priestess, and the entire future royal staff. Half the Priestess caste vying for her appointments…"

"You do have her problems," Dallan said, interrupting her.

"Oh, that's right, I do," Rika said with pleasure. Her thoughts were pleasantly occupied for a moment, then a monumental thought struck her. "This might be perfect timing, Dallan."

"For what?"

"Senta returns within the week."

Dallan's eyes brightened at the prospect. "That's right," she said, "this could be perfect."

"Senta?" Lifa asked, "for Skye? But Senta keeps very much to her own cohort. Astrid hasn't openly said so, but Senta prefers the company of older women. I don't know that she's ever been with a younger woman, especially one as young as Skye."

"You didn't see the way Senta looked at Skye the day Skye kissed her at the Academy," Rika said, remembering Senta's enigmatic expression, one that Skye had missed, but one that she and Dallan had easily interpreted. "That was a promise if I've ever seen one."

"A guarantee," Dallan agreed, "that there would be consequences to Skye's little stunt."

"Really?" Lifa said with growing excitement. She remembered the story well, how Skye had helped Dallan's team in field exercises, capturing a flag no one thought obtainable. Senta had caught Skye at the last minute, literally lifting her from her feet to keep her from the prize, but Skye had startled her by kissing her. And although Skye had been vague on how things had proceeded, it was evident that Senta, at least initially, had returned the kiss. And by Dallan's and Rika's account, Senta had given Skye a searing look at the end of that day, then simply walked away. Lifa herself recalled some pleasant tension between the First General and Skye when Skye had playfully challenged her after an archery contest.

"Has Senta seen Skye since the Academy?"

"No," Dallan said, "Not really. She returned briefly when Skye was ill and unconscious, but she left almost immediately to invade the Garmlain territory. She's been on campaign ever since."

"This is perfect," Lifa agreed. "I'll wait until Senta gets resettled, then see what I can do."

Skye spent the night in Ama's arms, giving the little Priestess renewal as much as she gave to Skye. It was one of Lifa's little secrets, when she had a Priestess who was tired or in need of rejuvenation, she scheduled

Skye to see her, for Skye enjoyed giving as much as receiving. Although all Ha'kan were sexually generous, Skye was especially so. Rika enjoyed a vigorous night with Lifa, replete with role play and acrobatic positions, sating them both completely. Dallan, on the other hand, spent the night performing her royal duties which consisted of a formal dinner with her mother and the Queen's staff, followed up by a few hours spent with one of the daughters of the high-ranking nobility, a pretty enough young lady who screamed quite loudly when Dallan brought her to pleasure. Although Dallan enjoyed it as she did all sex, she gratefully retired to her own chambers to spend the rest of the evening alone. This did not quite happen as Kara saw her entering her suite by herself and therefore joined her for nothing more than slumber. And Dallan welcomed the presence of her future First Scholar, who wrapped her arms about her as she fell asleep, for the Ha'kan were rarely alone from the day they were born.

Chapter 3

The following hours passed quickly. Gimle would be returning within days, which Skye was looking forward to. Gimle's future successor, Kara, had continued Skye's education, providing lengthy albeit disorganized lessons which Skye eagerly absorbed. Her formal education had been interrupted by the war and now she vowed to continue it. Kara was brilliant and had adapted to Skye's aural style of learning once she realized Skye, although a poor reader, could remember everything she heard. These lengthy tutoring lessons often ended with Skye tied to Kara's bedposts as she conducted whatever random, sexual experiment struck her fancy, and the Ha'kan society as a whole benefited from Skye's willingness to be Kara's experimental subject.

But Gimle was a mage, talented in an area where Kara was not. Kara was the future First Scholar, but Gimle was the current First Scholar, a premiere member of Queen Halla's staff. And although Skye would never have guessed she had any magical ability, Gimle was slowly but surely bringing it forth. Magic tended to follow the path of the practitioner's existing skills, and Gimle was a healer and an inventor. Skye had yet to find her path, because although she was mediocre at everything magical, at least in her mind, she wasn't really good at anything. Gimle, on the other hand, thought it extraordinary that Skye could dabble in any type of magic, destructive, natural, mechanical, or otherwise, and somehow make something work.

"By the gods, you're deep in thought."

Skye looked up to a pair of flashing dark eyes. Her heart, as always, gave a little leap at Dallan's presence.

"I was just thinking about Gimle, how nice it'll be for her to return."

Dallan zeroed in on the comment with precision. "Gimle? Do you want to have sex with her?"

"No!" Skye exclaimed. Both Dallan and Rika were quite occupied by Lifa's attempt to pair her with an older woman. "I mean yes, of course, your mother's staff are all mesmerizing. But no." She gave the idea some additional thought, then shook her head vigorously. "No, if she's anything like Kara, I think I'd be killed in the act."

"I don't disagree with you," Dallan said. "I've often found Gimle attractive, yet terrifying in a cerebral way. That said, will you join me in the garden tonight?"

Skye suddenly felt shy, an odd sensation since Dallan had been her first sexual experience and one continually since. "If you wish," Skye responded.

Skye did not know it, but that gentle reticence was an aphrodisiac to the Ha'kan. Their society was so open that even mild reluctance was foreign to them. Paradoxically, combined with the sexual passion the Ha'kan themselves shared, it was irresistible.

"Then meet me outside my doorway to the garden, around 7th bell."

Dallan was waiting for her when she arrived just before 7th bell. She wore beautiful, casual clothing for lounging. For the Tavinter, clothing was merely utilitarian, but Skye had learned that for the Ha'kan, it was a form of communication in and of itself. There was elaborate formal wear, there was clothing designed specifically for training, and there was armor for warfare. There were shirts and pants appropriate for the classroom, and there was casual wear made for relaxing with one's friends. And then there were the ensembles designed specifically for intimacy, ranging from the robes that intimated possibilities to the sheer gowns that informed you that you would be on your back within minutes. Dallan wore something in between, something that indicated Skye would be casually seduced but that the end result was not in question. Skye had no idea what to wear and thought most times she would be better off showing up naked, a suggestion greeted enthusiastically by all her companions. So, she allowed Lifa or surprisingly Kara, to dress her, and both succeeded in translating her intentions, even those she was unaware of.

Dallan looked at Skye with appreciation. The slender Tavinter could make even the drabbest clothing look good, but the lounging wear she had on now was elegant and flattering. Dallan was not certain why she bothered, because the better Skye looked, the sooner that clothing was coming off of her.

"Can I show you the gardens?"

Skye nodded and took Dallan's outstretched hand. The Ha'kan Princess walked her through the many paths, the twists and turns of the well-manicured grounds. And although it was far more domesticated than Skye was used to, she loved the trees and flowers of the natural world. Dallan watched her, enamored, as she absorbed every detail of the flora and fauna. She had known Skye would love this garden.

"It's beautiful," Skye said, breathing in the smell of the grass, the scent of the flowers. Even the trees gave off a powerful pine smell which Skye had found lacking in most domesticated settings.

"I thought you would like it here," Dallan said. "It's not your home, but it's the closest we have to it."

The Ha'kan princess was beautiful in the moonlight and Skye felt her heart beat faster. Still, she was reluctant.

"There's no one here," Dallan promised. "I wouldn't do that to you without your permission." She took Skye into her arms. "This just reminds me of your first time, by the stream."

Skye had to agree. Her first sexual experience had been with Dallan, unplanned and unsupervised in a decidedly non-Ha'kan way. They had been on field exercises with Skye soundly trouncing both Rika and Dallan when Dallan had come across Skye and seduced her right out of a tree. Their ensuing passion had been marvelous, but Dallan had regretted the situation, wishing something more perfect for Skye, something with a soft bed, incense, silken sheets, and candlelight. But even when Dallan had given her that experience weeks later at her Age of Consent, Skye never regretted the initial experience. For a Tavinter, born of the forest and one with the natural world, it had been perfect.

And it was perfect at the moment. Dallan was dazzling, her dark hair pulled back and her dark eyes black in the dim light. She looked at Skye with love and desire and Skye returned both emotions. Although never exclusive, she and the Ha'kan Princess had shared a powerful bond from the day they met, and it was perhaps even more powerful by that lack of exclusivity. Skye was connected to everyone who was tightly bound to Dallan as well.

"I missed you so when you were gone," Dallan said, a catch in her voice. She pulled Skye to her and kissed her, the lips soft at first then harder, the tongue gently probing, then thrusting deeper. Her hands went beneath Skye's shirt, caressing the lean muscles of her stomach then trailing upwards to encircle the breast. The hand held the breast captive while the fingers took charge of the nipples which responded to their touch. The soft moan she elicited from Skye only inflamed her, and the other hand went to work, caressing the stomach muscles but traveling the opposite direction into Skye's pants where the fingers skillfully manipulated the tie at the waist then dove lower. This elicited more than a moan, more of a gasp as they touched the soft down between Skye's legs then caressed the warmth and wetness below. Skye pressed against her, wanting the hand to press harder, to go inside her, and the fingers complied.

"I want you to lie down," Dallan whispered to her, biting her earlobe as she did so, and Skye obeyed as Dallan gently guided her backward then down into a patch of soft grass. They were surrounded by beautiful flowers not yet damp with evening dew, and the ground was warm and dry. The fingers thrust inside her and Skye's hips came up in response while Dallan's tongue probed her mouth even deeper. Then the lips worked their way down her throat, nibbling on those sensitive spots, then continuing down to the breasts where they suckled contentedly for some time while the fingers stroked and thrust their magic. And when Skye thought she could not take any more, Dallan's thumb made a gentle but firm circular motion while her long fingers stroked in and out and the lips suckled the breast without pause. And Skye cried out as her hips responded to the lips, the thumb, the fingers, and to Dallan herself. Skye climaxed, the warm wetness between her legs a perfect complement to the warm earth below.

And Dallan let her rest for a moment, but not long, because then she whispered the words Skye knew would be next.

"May I use my harness on you?"

Because none of the Ha'kan, not even the Princess herself, would use the device of pleasure without permission. But Skye gave that permission, as she had every time, even implicitly when she had been Dallan's captive in the war. And Dallan donned the device skillfully, the Ha'kan toy that gave pleasure to both women, penetrating the one and providing that pleasant pressure that could bring the wearer to forceful climax. And she buried herself in Skye, thrusting her hips forward and bringing intense sensation to them both. And the fact that Skye had already climaxed once simply aided her entry for Skye was wet and the stroke was smooth. A skilled Ha'kan could drive her partner to orgasm whereas an expert could bring both to pleasure simultaneously so that her own climax drove that of her partner. And Dallan was indeed an expert as she built her own pleasure wave by wave, thrust by thrust, while pushing Skye inexorably towards that edge. And when at last she felt Skye begin to release, she herself abandoned herself to the sensation, driving deeply into her little Tavinter and wrenching a lengthy, shuddering orgasm from her while she herself climaxed on top of her. And in the end, both collapsed, exhausted and spent, completely sated.

"By the gods, I love to do that to you," Dallan whispered. "Even when I see you on the field in training, I want to take you to the ground."

"It's a wonder we accomplish anything at all," Skye murmured, drained.

"Mmm," Dallan agreed, bit her earlobe once more, then rolled her over so she was lying on her chest. Skye was not fragile nor particularly small, but Dallan always felt as if she would crush her, a feeling that, accurate or not, excited her.

"I want you to sleep with me tonight," Dallan said, a request that carried far more weight with the Ha'kan than a request for sex. The Ha'kan would have sex with one another without reservation, but they slept, as in actual sleep, with only those they loved.

"Of course," Skye said sleepily.

"Unlike you, I don't think I can sleep out here. Will you come to my chambers?"

"Of course," Skye repeated, even more drowsy. And she followed Dallan, who half-carried her, to the chambers of her royal highness where Skye fell into a gigantic bed while the future Queen of the Ha'kan wrapped herself about her beloved Tavinter and fell into a deep, peaceful sleep.

It was late, but Queen Halla was wide awake, her excitement palpable. She sat in the open forum that was at the center of the suites of her staff. It was a large, comfortable area with soft couches surrounding a fire pit filled with glowing embers. She, Astrid, and Gimle often met there to talk when they were discussing matters that were not too private. Dallan visited her there as well, and she enjoyed spending time with her lovely, charismatic daughter in front of the fire.

But tonight, she was there alone because she was waiting for someone special, and her heart took a little leap when she saw the tall, confident figure stride through the door. She stood, smoothing her royal robes, and the movement caught Senta's eyes, who stopped, surprised.

"Your Majesty," Senta said, pleased, "I didn't expect to see you this evening."

"Really, Senta," Halla said, chiding, "Did you think I wouldn't stay awake to greet the returning, victorious First General of the Ha'kan?"

The comment brought a smile to the reserved General's face. Her beautiful, sensual Queen wore garments that had two simple but related purposes. The first was to subtly reveal the curves of the lovely body beneath them and the second was to make the clothing easy to remove. Her eyes drifted down to the full breasts outlined by the sheer cloth, then further down the line of the curve of the hip. Without hesitation, she stepped forward and took the Queen in her arms, pulled her forcefully to her and kissed her deeply, parting her lips with her insistent tongue. Halla made a noise of pleasure deep in her throat, for she had so missed her First General. She could feel the muscles in Senta's back and ran her fingers along the muscles of her arms. Senta was always in outstanding physical condition and battle had hardened her physique further. Senta's lips left a trail of fire down her throat and Halla took that opportunity to speak.

"Are you tired from your journey?"

Senta's words were muffled by the top of the breasts she now had her lips pressed to. "All thoughts of sleep fled the minute I saw you."

"Mmm," Queen Halla, said pulling her First General towards her door, "then let me give you the proper greeting a Queen should give her victorious General."

Senta smiled once more as she followed Halla into her chambers. "If this is the reward," she said, closing the door behind her, "it's a wonder the Ha'kan don't stay at war perpetually."

Chapter 4

Skye was on the training field when she was approached by one of Lifa's staff, Freya, who attracted many admiring glances from the other women. Skye loved Freya, and her twin Leya, for they had taken her under their wings from her first days at the Academy. It was unusual to see her on the practice field, and her flowing Priestess raiment was a stark contrast to the leather and steel armor that everyone wore. Their brief meeting drew many eyes.

"Hello, Freya."

"Hello, Skye," Freya said, leaning forward and brushing a kiss on her lips. Skye blushed because although the greeting was not at all unusual within the Ministry walls, it really seemed quite anomalous on the training field, at least to her. She hoped Dallan and Rika weren't looking because she would never hear the end of this.

"Lifa would like to see you right now, if you have a minute to spare."

"I always have time for Lifa," Skye said, a bit concerned, "is everything all right?"

"Oh yes," Freya said, "it's a minor detail and will take but a few minutes. She just wants to see you now."

"Very well," Skye said. This was a strange request. Lifa was not one to interrupt her training without significant reason. "I'll come see her now."

"She's not in the Ministry building," Freya directed, "she's in the chambers of the High Priestess."

"Oh," Skye said, wrinkling her brow. This was all very odd, and the thought of going to Astrid's chamber made butterflies flit about her stomach. "All right, then."

She saw Dallan across the field and waved to her, and Dallan simply waved back. Skye was relieved but would have been far less so had she seen Dallan turn to Rika and grin as soon as Skye's back was turned. She started across the courtyard to the royal palace.

Lifa sat with Astrid within Astrid's antechamber and the two discussed plans for Senta's formal dinner. Senta sat off to the side, drinking some strong black tea and reading through Rika's reports regarding troop readiness. Everything seemed in order, although there was a gap of a few weeks where it appeared Rika was gone, which she would have to ask her about.

Senta wore a casual but fetching robe, and Astrid looked over at her with great love, admiring her strong, fine features. Senta had spent her first hours home on top of and reuniting with the Queen, which was highly appropriate. She then went to her own chambers and slept for a while. When she awoke, she spent several more hours in Astrid's chambers while the High Priestess expressed her joy at her safe return, primarily with her lips and tongue, dominating the powerful General in ways most would think impossible. Senta would spend the approaching evening with Gimle, and her homecoming would be complete as the Ha'kan royal staff was whole once more. Senta's legendary stamina ensured that the homecoming was accomplished in a single day, although truth be known, she could probably have finished it back-to-back in far less time. Right now, she was content to lounge about catching up on paperwork.

Skye wandered through the Queen's forum nervously. She saw the markings on the door associated with the Ministry, just like the ones on Lifa's door, and she assumed these were Astrid's chambers. She paused, gathered her courage, then knocked lightly on the door. One of Astrid's staff, another Priestess, opened the door and smiled gently at Skye, motioning for her to enter.

Astrid's chambers were lavish, like Lifa's, designed for comfort and pleasure, a delight to all the senses. She could see Lifa through another doorway and Lifa glanced up, motioning to her. Skye followed the direction and pushed her way through the veils. And she stopped.

Senta took a sip of her tea and set a paper to the side, picking up the next. The movement in the doorway caught her eye and she looked up. And she stopped.

Skye stared at the First General, whom she hadn't seen in years. Senta had always been beautifully handsome, overwhelming, larger than life. She could be incredibly imposing and even lounging about so casually in a robe, she cut a daunting figure. Skye felt an inconvenient twist somewhere in her midsection, and really, all she could think of at that moment was Senta holding her a foot off the ground and kissing her so deeply she had nearly swooned.

Senta stared at Skye. She really had not seen the girl since the Academy, and all the promise of that lovely child had been fulfilled in an almost ethereal beauty. Skye's light hair, hazel eyes, and tan skin had always been exotic to the Ha'kan, but now they were even more so. Her features were sharper, the refined cheekbones more pronounced, the lips as perfect as they always were. Senta allowed her eyes to leisurely travel Skye's lithe form. She was still slender, taller, a little fuller in the breasts but still slim through the hips. Her eyes returned to the hazel eyes and the tan cheeks that were now flushed a fetching shade of red.

Astrid looked up at Skye, caught her expression, then turned to look at Senta, who astonishingly, had a very similar expression on her face, although Senta's was far bolder and amused whereas Skye looked like she might flee the room were she not frozen in place. Astrid was amazed. The silent, heated exchange was extraordinary, unexpected, and it pleased her greatly.

"Hello, Skye," Senta said.

"First General," Skye said formally, swallowing hard. "Welcome home."

"Thank you," Senta said, her eyes once again leisurely examining her. "How are you feeling?"

"I'm well," Skye said, "I think I'm completely healed."

"Good," Senta said, and the two stared at one another a moment longer.

Skye was finally able to break free of the spell she was under and turned with some embarrassment to Lifa.

"You wished to see me?"

"Yes," Lifa said, pleased beyond words. "I wanted you to know we're having a formal dinner to welcome Senta home. It'll be tomorrow night and you're expected to attend."

"Of course," Skye said. Had she her wits about her, she would have thought it strange that Lifa had called her from training to deliver such a routine message. It did not seem that there was anything else required of her, so she nodded uncomfortably to Astrid in order to take her leave.

"High Priestess," she said respectfully.

"Skye," Astrid responded with a tender smile.

Skye went to leave but could not resist taking one last look over her shoulder at Senta, which she regretted for the woman's amused, searing gaze was still upon her. Senta watched her leave, then returned to her paperwork. The silence in the room grew pronounced, and without looking up, Senta at last spoke.

"Something on your mind, ladies?" she said drily.

Lifa jumped to her feet. "I have arrangements to finish. Thank you so much for your help. And welcome home, First General."

"I will see you out," Astrid said, also getting to her feet. She followed Lifa into the hallway, who was positively beaming. Astrid looked down at her apprentice with great love and admiration. She had been trying to get Senta to engage with a younger woman for years. It was part of Senta's responsibility, especially in her position of authority. Astrid had nudged, reasoned, chided, cajoled, persuaded, but Senta, who was dutiful in all things, had been steadfast in her lack of interest. And now it appeared her successor might address two matters at the same time.

"Well done," Astrid said with pride, "well done."

The formal dining room was resplendent with decorations and Queen Halla entered with anticipation. She enjoyed all revelry, but this dinner would be special as it was more private and intimate than the obligatory social functions. The guests consisted only of her immediate staff, Dallan, and Dallan's immediate staff.

Because Senta was the guest of honor, Halla assumed she would sit at her right hand, but Dallan rushed to that position, a place she was certainly entitled to. Astrid took her usual position at Halla's left, and Lifa sat next to her. Rika, as was her custom, was at Dallan's right. Kara and Gimle, who had been engaged all day in deep philosophical discussion on the ethics of utilizing magical spells to facilitate sexual pleasure, sat at the far end of the table, showing no signs of ending their conversation. That left only two seats open, one next to Lifa, and the one directly across from it next to Rika. Skye was one of the last to enter, and she took the place next to Rika. And as they all stood, waiting for the Queen to sit, it was with a small thrill and considerable discomfort that Skye observed Senta take the only remaining seat across from her. Although it was cool in the hall, she felt a little flushed and her eyes flicked upward to Senta, who was gazing down at her with considerable enjoyment, well aware of the maneuvering that was taking place in the hall.

Halla took her seat and drink and conversation began to flow. Dallan was particularly animated, entertaining her with stories and anecdotes. Lifa and Astrid added their usual vivacious contributions, and Rika was wickedly funny as always. Kara and Gimle were still deeply engaged in their separate conversation, but every once in a while, offered up a comment or insight that was on-point and generally hysterical. Halla became aware, however, that her guest of honor was contributing little, and she glanced down the table at Senta. She stopped in mid-sentence, astonished at the look on Senta's face, and followed her First General's intense gaze to the little Tavinter who looked as if she could warm the entire hall with the heat coming off her face. She leaned toward her High Priestess.

"Is there something going on right beneath my nose that I'm unaware of?" she said under her breath.

"Not yet, your Majesty," Astrid said, a smile playing about her lips, "but we're all hopeful."

Halla leaned back, suddenly understanding the random seating chart that had not been random at all. A smile played about her own lips as she observed the unexpected but welcome attention of her First General focused on the one seated across from her. The entire situation was welcome, and she was relieved that she was not as out-of-touch as she first thought.

Senta took pity on Skye and relieved her of the weight of her scrutiny, although she did enjoy looking at the girl, as well as the self-conscious response it elicited. She turned towards the Queen's voice as the dinner was served.

"So, Senta," the Queen said, "tell us how the war fared."

Senta took a drink of her wine, a wonderful red that complimented the rare, thinly sliced beef they were served.

"The Garmlain are utterly destroyed," Senta said, "their lands clear to the border of the empire have been taken. There are stragglers here-and-there, but as a people they've ceased to exist. We were approached by imperial troops when we neared the border as they were concerned about our intentions. I assured them we had no intent of expanding further and that our dispute was with the Garmlain and the Garmlain alone."

As she said this, she looked to Skye who had taken a great breath and released it. The Tavinter had suffered greatly at the hands of the Garmlain.

"And there were no problems with the imperials?" Halla asked.

"No," Senta said, "I spoke with the knight commander personally, a woman by the name of Nerthus. She was interesting, to say the least." That was a mild assessment, Senta thought, the woman was cold and arrogant, extremely large for a human, male or female, and she seemed quite threatened by the size of the Ha'kan, especially Senta who was large even for their kind. Senta enjoyed towering over the woman and noted how quickly she got back on her horse. "I assured her we were finished with war for the time being. She asked about the Tavinter, and I told her that our people had made a lasting peace, even to the extent that Tavinter scouts were incorporated into Ha'kan forces, a claim she met with disbelief."

"Did she express any other concerns?"

"It was not so much a concern, but she did inquire about the trade routes that were previously held by the Garmlain. I informed her the routes were now in possession of the Ha'kan, but that we were open to negotiating their use for the good of commerce in Arianthem."

Halla nodded, greatly pleased with the diplomacy of her First General. The trade routes were valuable. The Garmlain had been a greedy and corrupt people, dominating commerce throughout the region. The trade routes, if leveraged properly, could bring about great goodwill in addition to prosperity, something that would only add to the stability of the region. Relations between the Ha'kan and imperials had been cool at times, always respectful but wary, two mighty nations of equal power but widely culturally divergent.

"Your skill in battle is matched only by your skill in diplomacy," Halla said, raising her wine goblet, "to the First General of the Ha'kan."

"To all the Ha'kan," Senta added, and they all drank the toast. Senta tipped her glass to Skye, "and to the Ha'kan's newest allies," and they drank again.

Senta sat her goblet back down. "That brings up something else of interest. I passed an Alfar procession on my return from the imperial border."

Three heads came up simultaneously. Dallan's movement was subtle and Rika's only slightly less so. Skye, on the other hand, was terrible at deception, and her head jerked up conspicuously. She looked about the table, but no one saw, or so she thought until her eyes came about to Senta, who gazed at her markedly. The First General's eyes flicked to the other two, who were studiously examining the food on their plates.

"The Alfar?" Halla exclaimed, "Here?"

"Yes," Senta said, her eyes still on Skye who shifted in her seat. "It seems the Alfar have come down from their mountain on a diplomatic mission. It was quite an impressive procession, so apparently, they're very serious. I spoke with the ambassador who said they were on their way to the dwarves, then would engage the imperials. She also said they wished to meet with us very soon."

"That's strange," Halla said, "they have an embassy here in the capital, yet we rarely hear from them." The high elves were a proud and ancient people who generally regarded other races as inferior. They tolerated the imperials and held the Ha'kan in only slightly higher regard.

"This ambassador seemed quite high in their elven hierarchy, so something important is on their mind."

Skye shifted once more, much to Dallan's consternation, and Senta had enough.

"Why don't you tell me how and when the three of you came across the Alfar?" Senta said, looking from one to the other.

Dallan glanced at Rika, then quickly responded because Skye would sink them all. She had meant to speak with her mother, to tell her the truth about their latest escapade, but she had not found the right moment.

"Skye had some business to take care of in Tavinter territory, and we came across their procession on our journey."

Senta's gaze swiveled back to Skye, who stared at her food.

"Skye?" Senta said expectantly, "And just what type of business did you have to take care of?"

Skye looked up with resignation.

"I had to help steal an enchanted stone from that sorceress, Ingrid," she blurted out.

Dallan buried her head in her hands and Rika burst out laughing. She did not expect Skye to lie, but there were so many better ways that could have been said.

"What?" Halla exclaimed. She turned to her daughter. "Dallan! You said you were on vacation!"

"I was going to tell you," Dallan said defensively, "I just hadn't found the opportunity."

"And it was something of a vacation," Rika said, "it was fun." She had spent half the trip drinking in a tavern in Trygg, and the other half killing some Garmlain.

Halla turned her motherly fury on Rika, who straightened with alacrity. "Don't think you'll get off lightly in this," Halla said, "you've always been like a daughter to me and I hold you to the same standard as Dallan."

"Yes, your Majesty," Rika said, and it felt like she and Dallan were eight years old again.

Senta's eyes had not left Skye. There was far more to this story. "And what prompted this little excursion?"

"Raine asked for my help," Skye said.

"Raine?" Halla said, her tone rising even more, "the dragon's lover? Why did she not come to me? The Ha'kan are sworn to Talan's service."

"She didn't ask for the Ha'kan," Dallan explained, "she asked only for Skye. Skye wasn't even going to tell us, but you see how bad she is at hiding things. Rika and I forced it out of her; then we couldn't let her go alone."

"That was dangerous," Halla said, "you are the Ha'kan heir and shouldn't be gallivanting about the country on foolish adventures."

"Mother, I was at war for three years and commanded an entire regiment."

"That was different!" Halla said angrily, that anger that all mothers feel when their children are in danger. "You were surrounded by thousands of Ha'kan, not on your own facing the woman who nearly killed Skye." She looked down the table at the Tavinter. "Skye is the leader of her own people and I can't dictate or control her actions. But you're my daughter and you will not do such foolish things without my knowledge and permission."

Dallan was growing angry, and it seemed the conversation might escalate further, so Skye interjected.

"This is my fault," she said quietly. "But Raine asked for my help, and I owe her my life. And, quite frankly, none of us were in any danger as long as Raine was with us."

The girl's simple words calmed Halla. Senta leaned back in her chair and crossed her arms over her chest, spoke.

"I'm inclined to agree. Raine is a force to be reckoned with, and I don't believe she would place any of you in danger she couldn't protect you from." She would not let Skye off completely, however, and stared at the little beauty across from her, gentle but stern.

"I understand you're to assume command of the scout regiment before too long. That means you'll be under my command and part of my staff, so although Queen Halla can't dictate or control your actions, I certainly can."

Although Senta was serious, the sexual undercurrent between the two gave her words an unintended meaning that drew everyone's attention. And perhaps it was not entirely unintended, because Senta's eyes lingered on Skye's lips.

"Do you understand me?" Senta said, "You'll not do such things without informing your command."

"Yes, First General," Skye said, swallowing hard.

Halla gathered herself, realizing she had overreacted, although she was still upset Dallan had not been up front with her.

"I just wish you would tell me these things."

Dallan relented as well. "I wanted to, it just happened so fast and we were afraid Skye would disappear. You know how she is," she said in mock accusation, looking down the table at her.

Skye frowned back. How had this been laid at her feet? "Next time I'll just leave," she muttered.

"There won't be a next time," Senta reminded her.

"Yes, First General."

Lifa at last spoke. "Well, I for one would love to hear the entire story."

And so, haltingly at first, then with growing rapidity, the full story came out. There were a few omissions. For example, Dallan did not volunteer that she now counted the head of the Guild of Thieves among her friends, but the three managed to recount the majority of their adventure to the great entertainment of all at the table.

Chapter 5

A small contingent of Ha'kan cavalry, led by Senta, Dallan, Rika, and Skye, rode out to the edge of the forest. As a child, Skye had ridden horses only bareback, but she had gradually gotten used to the saddles and trappings the Ha'kan used. She made the adjustment for the sake of consistency within the regiment, not because she felt it gave her any more control over the horse. To her mind, the animal would go where it willed, so she always negotiated with the beast prior to mounting it. Most of the troops found this humorous until they saw that Skye's horse would do things no other animal would, and soon they, too, were speaking to their mounts prior to riding.

They reached the edge of the forest and the meeting area was empty. Birds chirped, leaves rustled in the gentle breeze, but there was no one around.

"I thought you said your regiment was going to meet us here?" Dallan said. She was expecting two hundred or so Tavinter and the place was empty.

Skye grinned. "They are here," she replied, and made a gesture in sign language.

Suddenly the forest came alive. Things that looked like trees turned in place, grew legs, and walked. Patches of grass stood upright, brushed themselves off, and started towards their leader. Branches in the trees above unfolded from their supine position and lowered themselves, dropping to the ground. Within seconds, over two hundred Tavinter materialized from their camouflaged positions, appearing out of thin air.

Skye approached Torsten who was grinning broadly. Dallan watched as Skye greeted her second in command, pounding him on the shoulders. "I will never get used to that," she said under her breath.

Senta also observed the feat with appreciation. She had battled the Tavinter far longer than Dallan, for years engaging in skirmishes over disputed borders. They were not a large or numerous people, but their stealth and skill in the forest was magical. Gimle had speculated that the Tavinter were not fully human, that at some point in time in the far past, elves and humans had produced offspring, resulting in the nomadic people.

"Skye!" Torsten said, deliriously happy to see his leader and friend. Others crowded around as well, proud and excited to see their beloved leader.

"You were wise to suggest the Tavinter join the Ha'kan forces," Dallan mused, speaking to Senta. "It solved so many problems and kept Skye from having to choose between her people and the Ha'kan."

"Yes, and kept you from having all your trysts in some pile of leaves in the forest," Senta said, knowing that Dallan would never have let Skye go.

And your trysts as well, Dallan thought, but was not so brave to voice the entertaining thought. She went to greet Torsten, as did Rika. They had enlisted Torsten's help to rescue Skye from the sorceress, and the skilled scout had impressed them with his loyalty and bravery.

It had been agreed that the Tavinter would remain most of the time in their treasured forest. Skye would split her time between the Ha'kan capital and her people, tending to her duties with both. The Tavinter regiment would train the majority of their time within their own ranks, sharpening the very specific skills that the Ha'kan needed from them. And then part of the time, the Ha'kan forces would train together with the Tavinter so they could mesh as a whole. Already, Ha'kan units rode out with three or four Tavinter advance scouts, and the forest rangers were rapidly garnering the admiration of those they had not yet won over. Anyone who had been with Senta's forces in the latter part of the war were already aware of the Tavinter abilities as the rangers assisted in bringing down their hated enemy, the Garmlain.

Because the Tavinter lived a far harsher life than the Ha'kan, most of their training was practical in nature, serving purposes such as providing food for their villages. For that reason, their training might have looked disorganized or even random to more traditional military minds. But one only had to spend time with a group silently tracking a bear, or bringing down an enormous elk, or wordlessly communicating with one another as they set a trap for one of the great panthers that roamed their lands, to appreciate how valuable that practical experience was. Dallan did get angry at Skye when she used herself as bait for a pack of Hell Hounds that had become separated from their Hyr'rok'kin cohort. She felt a chill down her spine as Skye came crashing through the forest with the horrifying beasts on her tail, but the entire thing had been orchestrated to perfection by the Tavinter who brought the monsters down as Skye scrambled into a tree, safely out of reach, laughing with exhilaration. Senta merely shook her head. She was well-used to the reckless nature of the Tavinter, a streak that was pronounced in Skye. She would, however, talk to her later about the stunt.

The few days spent with the forest people convinced Senta they needed little formal training. Their lives were built around sustaining the skills that allowed them to survive, and so training permeated every aspect of their day. A Ha'kan could spend the day in some leisurely pursuit whereas such a course of action would probably get a Tavinter killed. No, it would be a better use of time to work on the integration of the forces, something that could be done on a smaller scale. Still, the days spent in the forests had given her a renewed appreciation of her former enemies, as well as given her some ideas how to best use their skills. To her mind, it was a very productive journey.

Chapter 6

The Royal Guard lined up for archery exercises. The catapults were loaded, and the small tar and hay targets were loosed. Arrows began flying, some missing, many hitting, the moving targets. Skye watched the first round, waiting her turn with anticipation. This exercise mimicked a contest that had been held at the Academy, and it was far more challenging than standing before a static target and firing down range.

"Hey Dallan," Rika said, "who am I?"

Skye braced herself, for they were again making fun of her. Rika drew her bow, pointed it straight downward and fired it into the earth where the arrow stuck between her own feet. Dallan burst out laughing.

"No, it was more like this." She aimed off in a random direction and shot the arrow high into the sky. It sailed over Senta's head and off into a field, and the First General turned to give the Princess a stern look.

"Shut up," Skye said. "Does anyone want to wager on this activity?"

"No," Dallan said without hesitation.

"Not a chance," Rika replied, much to Skye's disappointment.

"Next rotation!" Senta called out.

The three walked to the line. "It would be better if both we and the targets were moving," Skye said, "we really should be doing this on horseback."

"Don't suggest that," Rika said. "At least until I've had the chance to practice without others watching."

"I think I'll suggest it first chance I get," Skye said, and loosed an effort which impaled a flying target. Dallan, although she had seen Skye do this on many occasions, was still impressed. Even the Royal Guard walked to the line with great concentration, patiently lining up their shot. Skye walked up and fired with barely a look, as if it were inevitable the target would fall. And it always did, for Skye never missed. Although Dallan and Rika were excellent archers, impaling far more targets than most, Skye casually brought down their number combined, the whole time musing to herself how to make the exercise harder.

Because of the trajectories of the targets, it was easy to see when someone particularly skilled was on the line. Skye became aware that someone to her right was bringing down a great many targets at a consistent pace. She peered down the row of archers and saw that it was Senta. Dallan stopped to watch as well, then saw an impish look appear on Skye's face.

"Skye," Dallan said warningly.

Skye notched an arrow in her bow and paused, giving far more attention to her shot than usual. She waited for something, what it was, not clear, then sharply swiveled to the right and loosed the arrow, then swiveled back so she was pointed down range.

Senta stared in consternation as her arrow flew cleanly down the field. She had missed one. She never missed one. And oddly, that target appeared almost to change course at the last second, as if it had been struck by a gust of wind. She snorted. How many times had she heard that excuse from recruits? She notched another arrow and took aim.

Rika stopped, for Dallan appeared to be choking on something. She thought at first she was laughing at her, but then knew she was not the object of Dallan's hilarity.

"Skye," Dallan said, "I'm warning you, don't do this."

Skye stood at the line, a picture of concentration. But then she swiveled sharply to the right, loosed the arrow, then swiveled sharply back, pointed down range. Rika tracked the arrow, astonished, for it struck a target down the line, redirecting it. She gasped when she realized what Skye was doing, and could barely contain her mirth. No wonder Dallan was choking.

Senta stared at the missed target again. This could not be possible. She never missed. And she certainly never missed two in a row, no matter how windy it was. She glanced to the flags to determine wind direction, and they hung limply, for there was no wind at all.

"Skye," Rika said, joining in on Dallan's warning, "you're playing with fire."

"Just one more," Skye insisted, "and then I'll stop."

Senta notched another arrow, took careful aim, and went through the motions as if to fire. But she did not finish the shot. Instead she held the arrow and watched as another arrow flew in from an odd angle, redirecting the target she had intended to bring down. She lowered her bow and looked down the firing line.

"Uh, oh," Skye said, and both Dallan and Rika took a large step away from her. Her cheeks grew instantly hot, but still she could not hide the merriment in her eyes. Senta, for her part, felt the twin emotions Skye often inspired in her, exasperation and admiration. The skill required for Skye to identify which target Senta was aiming for, the ability to time her shot so it struck just before Senta's, and the proficiency to redirect the target as intended were all dumbfounding. She looked at Skye with an enigmatic expression, one that was not enigmatic to Dallan or Rika because they had seen it on Senta's face before.

"Boy, are you in trouble," Rika said.

"I'm certain she knows it was just a prank," Skye said doubtfully.

"Hmm-mm," Dallan agreed, not at all convinced.

Skye placed her bow on the rack in the armory. Hers was slightly different from the standard Ha'kan bow, lighter but a little longer, a good compromise between a short bow and a long bow. With her skill, she could fire as quickly as a short bow but with as much power and distance as a long. If she needed great distance, she would move to the longer weapon, but she preferred her own.

Although she heard nothing, her instinct told her she was no longer alone, and she turned. Senta towered over her. Skye hoped Senta wasn't angry with her, but Senta didn't seem angry at all. She had a curious mixture of emotions on her face: the calmness and imperturbability she always possessed, a trace of amusement, a gentle sternness that told Skye she was indeed in trouble, and something else Skye couldn't quite identify.

"That was quite a little stunt today," Senta said.

"It was just a prank," Skye said. "I didn't mean anything by it."

"Hmm," Senta said, accepting the excuse not at all. "You played a prank on me at the Academy, do you remember that?"

"No," Skye said swallowing hard, and Senta leaned closer.

"Dallan is right, you're a terrible liar. Let me refresh your memory. It was on field exercises when you went to capture the flag on the back of Skull's Pass."

"Oh," Skye said, "that one." She was very aware of how close Senta was, that they were nearly touching.

"I was just a child," she said, sounding lame even to her own ears.

Senta settled her hands on Skye's hips, causing her to start, and she leaned down to whisper in Skye's ear. "You're not a child anymore, are you?"

"No," Skye said softly, although at the moment she very much felt like one.

"Do you know what I wanted to do to you that day?" Senta said, just as softly.

"No," Skye said.

"Here, let me show you."

And with that, Senta lifted Skye clear off the ground and pressed her back against the wall. She pressed the full length of her body against Skye, pinning her and holding her tight. She took possession of Skye's mouth with her own, burying the tongue deep to where it toyed and played with Skye's, subjugating it completely. The kiss took Skye's breath away and made her arch with longing toward the woman holding her. She wanted Senta to take her to the ground, all thoughts of privacy gone. But the kiss went on and on until Skye could feel the wetness between her legs as her need grew in proportion to the skill of that mouth. She literally ached with want and her head grew light with the passion that was increasing without release.

But then Senta pulled back, set her on her feet, and let her go. She looked down at her with that inscrutable expression, her eyes dark. "That," she said emphatically, "is what I wanted to do to you."

She turned on her heel and started for the door.

"Is that all?" Skye said, startled at the words coming from her mouth.

"Is that all you wanted to do to me?"

Senta stopped. She wondered how courageous the girl would be and she had not been disappointed. She turned around, her strong, fine features defined in the soft light.

"No," Senta said, "Not even close." She stared at the girl in front of her, knowing they were taking a step on a path from which neither could turn back. But she had started down that path long before that fateful day of field exercises, in truth she had started down it the first day she had seen Skye. "Why don't you come to my chambers tonight, around seven?"

Skye was numb. "All right," she said, "I'll be there."

Lifa had taken one look at Skye's dazed expression, then told both Dallan and Rika, utilizing her full priestess authority, to leave her alone. That had already been their intent, for they knew what was going to happen the minute Senta had turned down the firing line with that look on her face. It did not stop them, however, from engaging in quiet, wild speculation as to what Skye was about to experience.

Skye sat in her chambers until the three-quarter hour, then started the long trek towards the Queen's forum. Thankfully, no one was in the hallways other than a few attendants, and it was not long before she stood before the double doors that bore the markings of the Warrior caste, much like those on Rika's door. Her mouth felt dry. She took a deep breath and knocked quietly on the door.

The door opened and a servant greeted her, ushering her in. Senta sat before some paperwork and looked up at Skye's arrival. She nodded to the attendant, dismissing her.

"You may go," she said, and the servant left.

Skye stood there uncertainly as Senta's eyes took in every inch of her slender form.

"Come here," Senta said. Skye obeyed, and as she approached, Senta stood and took her hand. With no preamble whatsoever, she led her into the bedroom. She turned to Skye, unbuttoned the buttons on her robe, undid the sash at her waist, then dropped Skye's clothing to the floor. Senta's expression was so calm, so unperturbed, her actions so methodical, Skye wasn't certain she was having any effect on her at all. But Senta's sharp intake of breath told her that perhaps she was.

Senta's hands went to the soft, caramel skin as she ran her fingers from Skye's shoulders down her arms. The caress was so light and skilled it hardened Skye's nipples instantly, and Senta took in the sight of them with pleasure. The breasts were beautiful, firm, full, not large, for nothing about Skye was large, but perfectly proportioned. The soft hair between her legs was the same light color as that on her head. Senta had barely touched her, but Skye felt the touch of her eyes as surely as had they been fingers running endlessly over her body.

With that same, methodical intensity, Senta undid the sash of her own robe and dropped her clothing to the ground, and now it was Skye's turn for a sharp intake of breath, for the First General had a beautiful physique and was a glorious specimen of pure physicality. And everything about Senta was larger than life, from her long limbs to those firm breasts that were proportionate to her size. Skye wanted to kiss that skin, to put her lips on every part of her body, especially the nipples that were just below her mouth, positioned so fortuitously due to the disparity in their heights. But she seemed frozen in place, which bothered Senta not at all because it was her intent to do exactly as she wished to Skye. She took each of Skye's hands in her own, curled the fingers about her palms, then gently but firmly guided her onto her back on the bed. She stretched Skye's arms above her head where she pinned them, causing a natural arch in Skye's back which thrust those beautiful little breasts skyward.

And then Senta began kissing her, much like she had in the armory, that slow, searing seduction that brought wetness between Skye's legs. And although Skye wanted to press upward against Senta, Senta would not let her and held her pinned down, touching hardly any part of her other than the wrists she held restrained and the lips she bruised with that endless kiss. Skye moaned in frustration but Senta was barely beginning and tortured her with just the kiss for an eternity. Finally, she moved to her ear, dallying for another eternity, then trailed a burning, biting, licking kiss down to her breasts. She toyed with them, teased them, circled them, and when finally she took a nipple wholly in her mouth, Skye writhed beneath her, certain she would climax on the spot, although still, Senta had not touched her beneath the waist, or even beneath her breasts. Skye began to understand that what was happening was something very different.

The playful torture of the breasts continued and Senta was so strong she was able to restrain both of Skye's wrists with one hand, leaving a hand free to cup a breast while the mouth and tongue played with the other. The hand and mouth would switch duties so that each breast received the full attention of both. And finally, at last that hand trailed downward to toy with the taut stomach muscles, the muscles that stood in bold relief because of the strain of the frustrated desire. The fingers traced them, the tongue followed their outline, and Skye wanted to beg Senta, to plead with her to put her mouth on her and put her out of her misery.

But she did not, instead the hand moved lightly over the wet, downy softness between her legs, making her jump as if shocked but not providing any relief. Senta chuckled, ever-so-lightly caressed the hair once more, careful to barely touch her. The hand stayed lower, but her lips came back to Skye's as she lightly kissed her.

"You're doing very well," Senta whispered as she gave another light, shocking caress. Skye made a desperate noise, and Senta again chuckled.

"I'd like to use my harness on you."

Skye stared at her in disbelief. If she put that thing in her, she would climax instantly. She would probably move her hips in such a wanton matter attempting to wring pleasure from that device, she would lift the First General right off the bed. Instead of voicing any of these thoughts, she heard herself reply calmly.

"Very well."

Senta made a murmured noise of pleasure and somehow was able to magically don her harness with only one hand while she still held Skye's wrists restrained. Clearly the Ha'kan women grew more skilled at every aspect of sex as they grew older. Senta positioned herself above Skye, now pinning a wrist with each hand once more, and stared down intensely into those hazel eyes. Skye wanted to look away, to close her eyes, to run from the unbearable intimacy of that gaze, but she could not and held Senta's eyes.

And then Senta thrust into her, a powerful stroke that might have been painful were Skye not so completely wet. But Senta thrust into her and simply stopped, staring down into her eyes with great pleasure as the phallus was buried deep inside the girl. Skye wanted to move, wanted to thrash beneath her, wanted to thrust her hips upward to greet the penetration, but she did not think she could move with Senta's weight holding her. And part of her did not want to move, did not want to lose the battle they were waging, for Skye at last understood that Senta could control her pleasure to an extraordinary degree and wanted to drive Skye without mercy. Senta pulled her hips back, then thrust deeply into Skye once more, and stopped. Each thrust sent waves of pleasure through Skye's very core, and each pause allowed the pleasure to subside so Skye would not lose control. But every time Senta pulled back, then entered her again, the peak of the pleasure would be slightly higher, building to a crescendo that Skye was certain would kill her if not soon released. Each time, Skye fought to catch her breath, to slow the beating of her heart, to maintain her composure, and each time she held Senta's gaze without breaking eye contact. And slowly but surely, the length of time between thrusts was decreasing, almost imperceptibly, but just enough so that it was getting more and more difficult for Skye to suppress the movement of her hips, harder for her to catch her breath, harder for her to keep her eyes open. Senta looked down at the nipples that were so hard it looked painful, and indeed it might as well have been for Skye was in agony. Senta thrust deeply once more and moved closer, looking into Skye's eyes, her lips hovering just above Skye's mouth so that they shared the same breath.

"Please," Skye whispered, pleading.

And it was all Senta had been waiting for, for her own pleasure had almost overwhelmed her. Her thrusts grew harder and deeper, and there was no pause now. Skye began climaxing almost immediately, and stunningly, the climax did not peak or wane in any manner but just went on-and-on. She was not certain if it was one long orgasm, or simply climax after climax, but clearly it seemed her body was not going to stop having been denied so long. And each wave of pleasure was unbearably intense, only to be replaced by one just as much so. And Senta herself was lost, having pushed herself to the very brink and now her only thought was of coming on top of this girl for perhaps the next hour as those lovely little hips thrashed beneath her completely out of control. Her body was fully pressed against the litheness beneath her, her own hips buried between Skye's legs as she rode her hard and long and without ceasing. And she cried out not just once but multiple times until every ounce of energy in her body was gone and she collapsed on the Tavinter who lay gasping for breath, stunned.

Neither moved for a very long time, and it took the entire extent for the pulsating inside Skye to diminish. She groaned when Senta pulled the phallus from her and Senta rolled over onto her back, pulling Skye on top of her. Neither spoke, because the air was too thick with the intensity of the experience. Senta took Skye's hand, and buried her face in her hair, pulling her close and making her feel safe so that she would go to sleep.

Senta sat drinking her morning tea, reading an intelligence report from the border. The Alfar and Dverger had quickly come to some sort of preliminary agreement, which was unsurprising. Although the elves and dwarves differed greatly in appearance, they shared a common heritage. The Alfar shared no such heritage with the imperials and she thought negotiations with them would take a great deal longer.

There was a light knock at the door and Astrid came in, which Senta had fully expected, wondering only why it had taken her so long. Astrid opened her mouth to speak, then caught sight of the sleeping figure in Senta's bedroom. Her mouth snapped shut as she leaned to peer into the room with no attempt at discretion.

"Are you going to let her sleep in your bed all day long?"

"She's earned her rest," Senta replied, taking a drink of tea.

Senta's tone was very matter of fact but it thrilled Astrid. She was about to demand full details, claiming her prerogative as priestess, when another light knock was at the door, followed by the entrance of the Queen. Halla stopped when she saw Astrid and they looked guiltily at one another.

"Astrid," the Queen said formally.

"Your Majesty," Astrid replied.

"Senta," the Queen said just as formally.

"Your Majesty," Senta replied.

Halla started to speak, but she, too, caught sight of the naked figure entangled in the sheets of Senta's bed. She stared for a moment, processing this most excellent sight. She then completely trumped Astrid's prerogative.

"Senta, as your Queen, I command you to tell me everything."

Astrid burst out laughing, because really the two of them were acting like Academy school girls. Senta cast a glance over her shoulder into the bedroom when she heard movement.

"I think you woke her up," she said with mild reproof.

Skye was scrambling for her clothes. She had heard voices and she sincerely hoped that wasn't the High Priestess, as she suspected. She took one longing glance out the window, wondering if a fall from this height would kill her. She took a deep breath, walked into the bedroom, and felt the heat rise off her cheeks because it was far worse than she had thought.

"Your Majesty," Skye said stiffly.

"Skye," Queen Halla said.

"High Priestess," Skye said, also quite stiffly.

"Skye," Astrid said.

Skye turned to Senta who was looking at her with all sorts of amusement. Skye bowed to her rigidly. "First General," she said, then made as if to leave.

"Skye," Senta said with exasperation, "come here."

Skye moved uncertainly toward her and once she was close enough, Senta reached up and pulled her down by her shirt front, then kissed her very gently. "We'll speak later."

Skye nodded, and gratefully took her leave. Astrid observed the kiss with delight, because although gentle it was also passionate. The door had hardly closed when she burst forth.

"And by 'later' do you mean again?"

"If you're asking me if I would have Skye in my bed again, the answer is yes. If she wishes."

Halla was also delighted. It had been her hope that the two would simply have an enjoyable experience, but for Senta to take the girl as a lover, now that would be extraordinary. She sat down next to Senta and poured herself some tea.

"As exalted as the First General is, I will not stand this insubordination any longer. I demand you relate every last detail to me and the High Priestess."

Senta chuckled and set her paperwork aside as Astrid also settled in. She could hardly disobey the edict of her Queen.

Although Skye should have been exhausted, she had a strange, pent-up energy and she could not bear the thought of spending the day in formal training. In fact, all she wanted to do was run. And, she realized, as the head of a Ha'kan regiment and the ruler of an entire people, she could do exactly as she wanted. And so, she did, stripping down to the bare minimum in clothing and running through the fields behind the palace, and then up into the mountains. She passed many outposts with Ha'kan guards, all who watched the figure with admiration for the Tavinter ran like the wind, and Skye was one of the fastest of all her people. And finally, when she ran as far as she could and reached the highest peak that was accessible, she turned around and ran the entire way back. She guessed it was mid-afternoon by the time she returned and so she went to her quarters, bathed, and because it would have seemed odd had she not, went to Lifa's.

She was early, for it was barely past third bell, but Dallan, Rika, Kara, and Lifa were already there. They lounged about, trying to appear casual, but greeted her eagerly. They then settled back into their forced, casual lounging while Skye sat staring off at nothing. Lifa pretended to read a book, but she kept looking over the top of the pages at Skye's distracted air. She hoped that Skye would catch her looking and therefore initiate the conversation, but that did not happen, as Skye was completely someplace else. She could stand it no longer.

"Skye, are you all right?"

"What?" Skye said, bemused. "Yes, of course I'm all right."

Lifa was not certain how to continue, or even if she should, but it was within her responsibility.

"Did you have a nice time last night?"

Skye still had a distant look, but a little smile played about her lips and Lifa relaxed.

"By the gods, yes," she murmured, "it was amazing."

Both Dallan and Rika released the breath they had been holding, and Kara was even less subtle.

"Oh, thank the Divine," she said, "we were all worried about you."

"Worried about me?" Skye said, puzzled. "Why?"

"It's just such an intense experience," Lifa said, "and then you were gone all day."

"I had to go run," Skye said, "you know how I am."

Dallan relaxed completely. That was a very good sign. Dallan was bursting with curiosity, though, and Rika, who normally would come to Dallan's rescue by grilling Skye without end, was disappointedly circumspect. Kara, thank the gods, leaped right into things.

"So, I must know, Skye. The First General's stamina is legendary, and Gimle has often marveled at her ability to control her pleasure. I have a theory that the intensity and length of the orgasm is directly proportional to the foreplay that precedes it. Was that your experience?"

"You make it sound so sterile," Skye said, "but yes, the longer you delay that gratification, the fiercer the end result."

"Really?" Rika said, fascinated. "I mean, how long?"

"Hours," Skye said. "It's a fine line, though, because you think you might die leading up to it."

"And do you think you might share some of these techniques with my Priestesses?" Lifa asked, silently including herself in that grouping.

"Of course," Skye said, "I don't think I'm up to it this evening, but yes."

Lifa was as delighted as her mentor with the results of the pairing. For this was exactly what was hoped would happen, that the younger would gain knowledge and experience which she then would share with her own cohort. Lifa inwardly admitted that she was also delighted for personal reasons, for she herself would get to experience the fruits of such knowledge.

Lifa was leaving Astrid's room after a meeting with her and the staff of the High Priestess. She nodded to Senta, who was leaving her chambers, and was surprised when the First General called to her.

"Lifa."

Lifa stopped and waited for Senta, nodding respectfully as she approached. "First General," she said politely.

"I'm assuming that Skye has spoken with you about the night we spent together."

They all had been grilling Skye endlessly about it for two days, but she needn't provide that particular detail. It was fully within her purview as a Priestess to discuss the event with Skye, and Lifa knew that was what

Senta was referring to.

"Yes, she did."

Senta appeared thoughtful. "Do you think Skye would wish to spend another night with me?"

"I think she would like that very much," Lifa said, carefully containing her excitement.

"Good," Senta said, "thank you."

Senta turned to leave, and Lifa called out after her, "Do you wish me to say something to her?"

"No," Senta said, "No, I'll ask her myself. It's just that—," she paused for a moment, then said, "It's just that Skye is so very young, and so very generous with herself. I didn't want to put undue pressure on her."

Lifa was very much in love with the First General at that moment, for Senta was utterly desirable and most would have simply seduced Skye right back into their bed. But Senta was as concerned with Skye's well-being as she was with her own pleasure, and that made her irresistible.

Skye approached Senta's chambers nervously, but with great anticipation. She had not expected any further attention from the First General and had greeted her invitation with such disbelief Senta mistook it for hesitation. Skye had stammered out an explanation, convincing Senta that it was not reticence but surprise, and the two had arranged to meet in Senta's chamber once more. And as previously, when Skye entered, the First General sat lounging casually, so elegant and handsome she took Skye's breath away.

Senta set her work aside, her gaze moving appreciatively to the slender figure in her doorway. She saw Skye regularly but was still getting used to the flame of desire the girl ignited in her. She had suppressed it when Skye had been younger, but now that it was allowed to burn unabated, it was very enjoyable, something she experienced with few beyond the Queen and royal staff.

"I was quite demanding with what I wished of you last time, so now it's your turn. What would you like to do?"

Skye stopped abruptly and looked at her almost with suspicion. "You would let me be on top?" she said with doubt.

"Of course," Senta said, "I enjoy that very much. Would you like to use your harness on me?"

Astonishment was on Skye's face. "By the gods yes," she murmured. "I mean no!" she said quickly, "I mean, not just yet."

Her indecision was engaging. Senta knew it was rooted in Skye's concern about her ability to satisfy her, although she herself had no doubt of that satisfaction. "Why is it you seem surprised?"

"Dallan and Rika never let me be on top," Skye said, frowning, "I'm always earth to their sky."

"Have you ever asked them?"

Skye's mouth opened, then abruptly snapped shut as she thought furiously. Surely it could not be that simple. "No," she said at last.

"Perhaps you should try that," Senta suggested.

The consternation on Skye's face made Senta want to laugh, but she controlled herself. "Enough of that," she chided, "now get over here."

Skye still did not believe that she was going to be allowed to do whatever she wished, but Senta waited for her instruction as Skye stood before her. Very slowly, Skye held out her hand, and Senta took it. Skye escorted her into the bedroom and Senta sat down on the edge of the bed. Still in a state of shock, Skye undid the buttons on Senta's robe and parted it. Senta had to control her urge to remove Skye's clothing because she was slow to do so herself, so enamored was she with the vision before her. After what felt an eternity, Skye undid her own robe and dropped it to the floor. Senta took in the sight with appreciation, then leaned back.

Any doubt or hesitation Skye had disappeared because all she could think of was putting her mouth on every part of that gorgeous body. And so, she did, slowly, searingly, exploring every inch. And Senta watched that light-haired head move down her body, fascinated, her eyes dark with desire. Skye acted with such innocence it was as if every time was her first time, not in the sense of awkwardness or inexperience but in the sense of her wonder and delight. Every response she elicited, every movement, every breath, every noise, filled her with pleasure, a pleasure that only increased the sensation she was bringing forth in her partner. And in a way, that innocent, generous exploration was as dominating as Astrid's consummate talent. And Senta could tell Skye had already taken her lesson to heart for she delayed putting her mouth upon her, circling and coming tantalizingly close then teasingly moving away. And when Senta thought she could take no more, Skye glanced up, a wicked glint in those beautiful hazel eyes, then put her mouth fully upon her, causing Senta to nearly climax at that moment. And Senta cradled that fair-haired head in her hands, watching in disbelief as that perfect mouth moved on her, the tongue lightly flicking and teasing, then probing. And so talented was that mouth, Skye did not even use her hands but rather placed them on Senta's hips which moved beneath her. And Skye loved every part of it, leaning her head to the side so she could look up without taking her mouth from its duties, taking in those magnificent breasts, the stomach muscles that tightened with each thrust of the hips, the eyes that looked upon her with such love and desire. And then Senta was climaxing, the hips no longer in any control, having fully submitted to the mouth that continued to skillfully prolong the orgasm. And it continued for an extraordinarily lengthy time, losing nothing to numbness or loss of sensitivity as could happen with a less skilled lover. No, Senta simply came until she could not do so anymore, and really it was her own limitations for Skye would have stayed upon her all night long.

Senta collapsed and Skye smiled, so happy was she for Senta's satisfaction. And Senta was so sated she pulled the girl close to her, intending to satisfy her but realizing she could not, at least not right now. Instead she just chuckled and kissed her.

"Now see, you've already assured our next pairing for I must repay such a performance, and I can't possibly do so now."

"You don't owe me anything," Skye said shyly. "I enjoyed that."

And Senta knew that she did, which made her own pleasure all the more intense and her satisfaction all the deeper. And she was quite content to drift off to sleep with the girl in her arms.

Chapter 7

kye was on her way to the Scholar's building. Today she would be working with Gimle and therefore would forego regular warrior training. She enjoyed her time with Gimle, she just didn't think she was very good at magic, and therefore she looked with a little longing towards the practice fields as she walked by. That was something she knew she was good at.

She caught sight of Rika and redirected her path. She had thought long and hard about this and had made up her mind. Now she steeled herself as she approached the future First General. Rika had her back to her and was giving instruction to one of the soldiers, so Skye waited until she finished. Rika ended the conversation, then caught sight of Skye.

"Rika," Skye said formally and just a touch awkwardly, causing Rika to grin.

"Something on your mind?"

"I was wondering if you had plans this evening."

Rika did in fact have plans with Lifa but was so intrigued by Skye's demeanor, she determined to change them. Lifa would encourage such a change, given the circumstances, but only if she were given a full report after the fact.

"No, not at the moment."

Skye thought she should just blurt it out. "Would you like to come to my chambers this evening?"

"I think I would like that very much," Rika said.

Skye took a deep breath. "Might I be on top?"

Rika grinned even more. "I was wondering how long it would take you to figure that out. Of course, you can."

"Good," Skye said, bright red from the roots of her hair. "Then I'll see you later."

Rika watched her go, entertained by the exchange and looking forward to the evening. Senta passed her, catching sight of her expression and then glancing to Skye's retreating back.

"You're welcome," Senta said, and Rika's grin just grew broader.

Skye drove into Rika with one last thrust before she collapsed on top of her. Rika actually trembled beneath her, laughing with pleasure and exhaustion. She stared up at the ceiling, enjoying the sight of those slim hips centered between her legs, the muscles in that beautiful back that were pronounced and heaving because of exertion. At the last minute she had talked Skye into coming to her chambers as an alternative, simply because she had an enormous mirror above her bed and could watch that pretty little backside at work. And work it did, for Skye had been saving up for this moment and unleashed a performance on her that was epic.

Skye struggled to catch her breath. She had pleasured Lifa and the other Priestesses on many occasions in this manner, but she had never experienced anything like that. No sooner had she donned her harness than Rika had snatched her close, and where her time with the Priestesses was passionate, it did not even feel like the same act. Rika was like riding a wild horse and their passion was almost violent. Rika bit her neck, both arousing and angering Skye, causing her to drive into the woman with abandon. She had fought to control the larger woman and succeeded only by completely sexually dominating her because there was no way she could have done it physically. And Rika enjoyed relinquishing all control to the sprite on top of her, marveling at the strength and stamina in that slender frame. And in the end, she had wrapped her long legs about Skye and raked her fingernails over her back, lifting her off the bed with the strength of her climax.

"I've injured you," Rika murmured, her mouth working poorly because it felt numb. "Your back looks like it was clawed by a bear."

This brought a little giggle from Skye. "Trust me, I didn't feel it."

"Even so, we'll have to get some salve from Kara. I don't want the Tavinter to declare war upon us because I killed their leader in bed."

Skye chuckled again and buried her face in Rika's breasts. She loved her smell, her taste, everything about her, and Rika felt that love and returned it, pulling her close. She remembered the very first day she had met Skye at the Academy, when she and that Pip character were at the archery range performing so poorly, Pip for real and Skye in ruse. On that day she had wanted to take Skye into the barn and put her on her back in the hay, and that desire had not lessened with time.

"By the gods, you're as talented with that thing as Lifa said."

"And why didn't you tell me all I had to do was ask?"

"Lifa told us not to. She said there were some things you had to learn for yourself."

"Hmmph," Skye said, "Then she'll be disappointed because I didn't figure it out for myself, Senta told me."

"But that's appropriate," Rika said, "it's Senta's role to teach you things even beyond what a Priestess could teach you. And then it's your job to share that knowledge with us."

"Which I gladly do," Skye said, adjusting her position and laying her head on Rika's chest so she could listen to her heartbeat. They fell into a comfortable silence and Skye wondered if Rika had fallen asleep, although she thought she was still awake.

"Can I ask you a personal question?" Skye said.

"That's funny, given our current positions. But yes," Rika said, "you can."

"The other night at dinner, the Queen said you were like a daughter to her, and I realized you've never spoken of your mother."

Skye was a little afraid the question might anger or even sadden Rika, but it did nothing of the sort. Rika grew reflective, but that was all.

"My mother was a great warrior, from what I'm told. Big and strong, one of Senta's cohort and most trusted staff when they were young. But she was killed in battle when I was very small."

"That must have been awful," Skye said.

"I hardly remember her," Rika said truthfully. "It was sad at first, but the Ha'kan are so communal, I was never alone, not even for an instant. And Dallan and I were already friends, but after that we became inseparable."

Skye tried to imagine Dallan and Rika as children, and it made her smile.

"So, although I lost my mother, I can't complain because I was surrounded by caregivers, Priestesses, other adult Ha'kan, and the end result is that I was treated like a daughter by the Queen herself, so I can't say I suffered greatly." Rika lifted her head slightly. "And what of your mother? I know of your father, Kolgrim, but I've never heard you speak of her."

"My mother's name was Isolde," Skye said. "She was amazingly beautiful, skilled at everything with a kind heart and generous nature."

Rika had to smile because Skye was speaking of her mother with great admiration but could have been describing herself.

"She was with me most of my life," Skye said thankfully, "but she grew very sick a few years before I came to the Academy. Not even Isleif could save her, and it broke his heart."

"The wizard seems very close to your family," Rika commented.

"Yes," Skye said, "I'm not really sure of the history behind it because Isleif is very old. But he's always been there when we needed him, and now I'm all that remains of my family."

"Hmm," Rika said, "I don't think you can reproduce by yourself like the Ha'kan, so we'll have to find some suitable man to breed you with."

"What?" Skye exclaimed, but it was such a Ha'kan comment, so practical about certain matters.

"Yes, and hopefully you'll have a girl which would solve a whole host of problems."

Skye hit her lightly. "You're not breeding me like some horse."

"All right," Rika said, rolling her over onto her back. "I'll keep trying, but I really don't think it works this way."

Skye's laughter bubbled over, right until the future First General kissed her and stopped their conversation for good.

Chapter 8

Skye spent a second day in the Scholar's wing working with Gimle, although right now Skye wasn't working but rather was staring at Gimle and trying to picture her and Senta in bed. Like all of the Queen's staff, Gimle twisted Skye into little knots with her willowy grace and dreamy, distracted sensuality. Skye could see Kara becoming more and more like Gimle each day, although Skye wondered if Gimle was as adventurous as Kara. The way she was looking at her right now, peering over those spectacles, Skye had the feeling she probably exceeded Kara in every category.

Skye started, realizing Gimle was staring right back at her, that benign, knowing look on her face. Skye went back to her studies, reading up on various spells. These were all boring, and she wasn't very good at any of them. Gimle had said that her magical abilities would parallel her natural ones, but Skye had yet to find a practical application where that was so. She was a good runner, and a good archer, and good with a sword, but none of these spells had anything to do with that. She could enchant an arrow or a sword, but generally the enchantment was so weak it was embarrassing. She had tried to enchant an arrow with fire, but nothing more than a few tendrils of smoke drifted from the shaft and she had thought angrily she could just thrust the thing into a fire pit and get better results.

She rubbed her eyes, wishing she were out on the training field with Dallan and Rika. Think, she demanded of herself. What was she good at? What was her gift beyond all others?

The answer came to her. She, like all of the Tavinter, was stealthy beyond reason. No one could hide and remain hidden like her people. This brought her thoughts around to her last escapade. The dragon, Talan, and her lover, Raine, had been seeking the enchanted stones to a fade bracelet, an artifact that would allow the dragon to pass through Nifelheim undetected. Skye had marveled at the possibilities, the ability to be not only stealthy but completely invisible.

There was a quill in front of her, a small, lightweight object. What if she could make it disappear? She stared hard at the quill, focused her energy as Gimle had taught her, concentrated on exactly what she wanted to happen...

And the quill disappeared.

Skye sat back, stunned. She looked about to make certain she hadn't simply knocked it to the floor, but it was gone. She was very excited and was going to call Gimle over, but then realized she could not prove what she had done. And had she really made it invisible? What if she had accidently sent it to another plane? Or what if she had just very quietly blown it up? She stared at where the quill had been, concentrating once more, focusing her energy.

And the quill reappeared.

Skye's excitement was enormous. She wanted to rush over to Gimle but wanted to make certain it had not been a fluke and that she could do it again. She stared at the quill once more, concentrated, and the quill disappeared. She reached out, hesitantly, to where the quill had been, and patted the area. Amazingly, she could feel the soft outline of the feather and the stiff end, so it was still there, it just could not be seen. She concentrated once more, and the quill came back.

"Gimle?"

Gimle looked up at her tone of voice. It was quiet, even a little uncertain, but something about it drew all her attention.

"Yes?"

"Can I show you this?"

Gimle walked over to her. "What is it?"

"Watch this," Skye said, and concentrated her attention on the quill. Once again, it disappeared.

"Was that sleight of hand?" Gimle asked.

"No," Skye said. "You told me to figure out what I was good at, and I am better at stealth than anything else. So, I thought if I can hide myself, what if I could hide other things?"

"Can you bring it back?" Gimle asked.

"I think so," Skye said, and once again concentrated. The quill reappeared and Gimle picked it up.

"That's extraordinary," Gimle said, holding the quill out. "Do it again."

Skye again focused her energy and the quill disappeared. Remarkably, Gimle could still feel the object in her hand, it just could no longer be seen.

"Amazing," she said.

A wave of exhaustion overtook Skye and the quill reappeared, even though that had not been her intention.

"Hmm, apparently I must maintain the spell to keep it invisible," Skye said, feeling a little light-headed. "That was very hard."

Gimle stared at the quill in her hand. It wasn't just hard, it was impossible. She had never heard of such an ability in any mage. She knew of certain spells that would cloud the mind, preventing someone from seeing what was actually there, and she knew many wizards, sorcerers, and witches who could use enchanted artifacts to travel through the different planes of existence. It was her opinion that was how the sorceress, Ingrid, had managed to disappear on two occasions. But traveling through Nifelheim was very dangerous, for the misty veil between worlds was full of dangerous demonic creatures. And no one could stay there for very long without risk of being trapped there forever.

But this was something very different. She felt no clouding in her mind and the object did not shift phases because it was still in her hand; she could feel it. It seemed that Skye had in fact turned the object invisible.

"Can you imagine," Skye said, "if I could turn myself invisible?"

"You will do no such thing," Gimle said sternly. "I need to do some research on this spell. Until then, you will not use it."

"Of course," Skye said, a little chastised, "I don't think I could do it on anything larger, anyway."

Gimle softened. "Skye, this is amazing. I've seen many things like this, but I've never seen anything truly turned invisible. I've never even heard of this ability. I just want to go through the library and make sure this is safe."

"I understand," Skye said, and she did, for Gimle always had her best interest at heart. "You know, I'm very tired and I think I would like to lie down."

"Why don't you go lie down in Kara's bed?" Gimle suggested. "I think you know where it is."

Kara came in a few minutes later and caught sight of the figure in her bed through the doorway. "Well, what do have we here?" she murmured.

"I think she's probably too tired for anything at the moment."

This was odd to Kara because it was very early in the day. "Did she have a full night?"

"No," Gimle said, staring at the quill she held in her fingers, "she turned this invisible."

"An illusion spell?" Kara said with interest.

"No," Gimle said. She was highly resistant to illusion spells or attempts to influence her mind. She would feel any attempt at such mental coercion. "I think she actually turned it invisible."

"How is that possible?" Kara said. Although not gifted with magic herself, she conducted a great deal of research for Gimle as the First Scholar was also the Queen's battle mage. "I've never seen or heard of an ability like that."

"Nor I," Gimle said. She was excited and intrigued by Skye's ability, but also concerned. "Would you help me search the archives to see if we can find something similar? I want to make sure that this spell is safe."

Hundreds of miles away, deep in the forest, a wizened, ancient wood elf sat before her fire in her cave. Elyara was at her side, and the two were quietly meditating. Raine would be there in a few days, responding to Elyara's request, and Y'arren was looking forward to seeing her friend and pupil. The wood elves worshipped the dragon, Talan'alaith'illaria, but her lover Raine was far more approachable and beloved to them.

Elyara wished to see Raine on a separate matter, one having nothing to do with the elves but rather events in the imperial capital. But now, Y'arren thought to herself, it was very good that Raine would be here soon. Something was stirring in the land of the Ha'kan, something of enormous power. And although she sensed it was little more than a child at play, that itself was dangerous. Because if she had felt that ripple of power, there were others far more dangerous and evil that undoubtedly felt it as well. And power such as that would draw all such creatures to it.

A stunningly beautiful woman came through the edge of the trees into the clearing, drawing the attention of the elves in the village. She wore lightweight leather armor with a bluish cast to it and bristled with weapons, but the smile on her face was as bright as the sun. That smile was instantly returned, and many ran to greet her. Raine hugged some, slapped the backs of others, clasped the forearms of the warriors, and lifted up children and spun them around while they squealed with joy. Y'arren heard the commotion and came out of her cave, accompanied by Elyara who also was all smiles.

Raine approached the diminutive seer, the powerful elven mage who was the matriarch of this clan. She went to one knee so she was on the same level as the ancient one, then hugged her. She stood, then gave Elyara a hug as well. The doe-eyed, dark-haired elf could barely contain her joy at seeing Raine.

"And did you walk?" Y'arren asked. "Where's your dragon lover?"

"I didn't walk very far," Raine said sheepishly. "Talan dropped me not too far away in the forest. Our goodbyes tend to be—," she cleared her throat, "passionate, and we thought it might be rude to carry on in the center of your camp."

Y'arren was so happy for Raine and it shined through in her ancient eyes. Raine was the offspring of two extraordinary races, a Scinterian father and an Arlanian mother. The Scinterians were mythic warriors, undefeatable in battle and the legendary allies of the dragons. The Arlanians, on the other hand, were a tragic race, a beautiful people who were destroyed because of their intense sexual desirability. They were fine artisans and musicians, but incapable of protecting themselves from the enslavement that resulted when they were discovered. It was an impossible pairing, for Arlanians could not reproduce except with other Arlanians, and Raine was an astonishing mix of the two, possessing her father's strength and ability in battle and her mother's beauty and passion in bed. Y'arren did not think Raine would ever find a suitable companion, and then she had found Talan'alaith'illaria, one of the twelve ancients and a queen among dragons. It was a perfect match, for dragons were a lusty lot but tended to grind their lovers to dust, whereas an indestructible Arlanian was a perfect solution to both.

"And where is your better half?" Raine asked Elyara, giving her a big hug.

"Dagna is in the capital. She's the official bard of the imperial realm, you know," Elyara said, a trifle facetiously, "and her duties are crucial to the function of the empire."

Raine grinned. Years ago, Dagna and Elyara had accompanied Raine on a dangerous mission to the Underworld that had stopped a Hyr'rok'kin invasion. It was on that quest, twenty years before, that Elyara and Dagna had met, and they had been inseparable ever since. They spent half the year in the imperial capital and half the year in the woods with Elyara's people. Dagna had immortalized their quest to defeat the Hyr'rok'kin in the epic poem, "The Dragon's Lover," and it had been wildly successful, solidifying Dagna's place in the literary world. Raine was just grateful she had left many details out so few could associate the heroine with her.

One of Y'arren's attendants motioned to them and Raine assisted Y'arren back into the cave where they sat down to drink some hot tea in the cool air.

"I met Feyden's sister not too long ago," Raine said. Feyden was one of the high elves, an Alfar who had also accompanied them on their quest years ago. "She's an ambassador and was on her way to see the dwarves."

"I had heard rumor of an Alfar procession," Elyara said, "and word has it they are next headed to the imperial capital."

"Yes," Raine said, "Maeva, I think that was her name, said they were going to negotiate with the Dverger, then with the imperials and the Ha'kan."

This mention of the Ha'kan caught Y'arren's attention and Raine looked to her knowingly. They would discuss that in a minute.

"Do you know what this is about?" Elyara asked.

"I'm guessing it's due to the increase in activity in the Hyr'rok'kin, and also due to Feyden's influence."

The mention of Hyr'rok'kin caused Elyara to gasp. "They've returned?"

"Not yet," Raine said. "We've seen only small pockets of them here and there, and a somewhat large contingent in the land of the Ha'kan a few years back. But even right now Talan is flying to the Empty Land to ensure they're not vomiting up out of the earth again."

"How can this be?" Elyara asked. "We shut the gate."

"Yes, we did," Raine said, "but the black dragon we defeated was not working alone. In fact, I believe he was answering to someone far more powerful."

"More powerful than one of the twelve ancients?" Elyara said fearfully. "More powerful than Talan?"

Raine was quiet for a moment. "Yes," she said, "more powerful than my love. But Feyden does what he can among the Alfar, and I'm certain the quick negotiations with the Dverger are a direct result of Lorifal's influence. I understand he's on the Dwarven High Council, now."

"Lorifal?" Elyara said in disbelief. The funny, crude little dwarf had been a valuable asset and ally on their quest, but it was hard to picture him in a position of authority.

"Oh, he's much the same," Raine said, laughing. "He still drinks and fights and lets loose wind from every orifice, but I believe those are all admired traits for the Dverger and probably helped him in his rise to the top. He and Feyden and I get together ever-so-often in some tavern somewhere, drink, and destroy the place in fine dwarven style." Raine was quiet for a moment, thinking of her friends. "And what of Bristol?" she asked, "and Gunnar?"

"Gunnar is a sad tale. I don't know that he ever recovered from the touch of the Membrane."

Raine's jaw clenched. The Membrane was a horrible creature, a smoky amalgam of limbs and appendages that perpetually pleasured and tortured itself. It was made of hapless victims it had seduced then absorbed, victims who were now doomed to an eternal, painful, endless orgasm. Its very touch poisoned one with fear and indecision, and it had wrapped itself about Gunnar. Raine was only able to rescue him by sacrificing herself, revealing to the creature her Arlanian heritage and drawing the monster away.

"It seemed he was destined for greatness," Elyara said sadly, "but he left the military shortly after our quest ended and now lives on a decrepit farm."

Raine sighed. Gunnar had been the leader of their expedition and it saddened her to know it had ended so badly for him. "And Bristol?"

"Bristol," Elyara said, "is in fact the reason why I asked you to meet with me. I think he would have come himself if he were not afraid what might happen in his absence."

Raine frowned. "What do you mean?"

"As you know, Bristol has advanced to a very high position in the imperial ranks. He now occupies the position of knight commander, and there are only two of those in the capital itself."

This somewhat made up for Gunnar's disaster. Bristol had been fearful, even cowardly on their mission, but in the end he had overcome his timidity and fought bravely. Raine had no doubt that Bristol would not have advanced much beyond his lowly position years ago had he not been forced to face his fears.

"Right. I believe the other knight commander is a woman?"

"Yes, Nerthus," Elyara said, and Raine could tell by her tone of voice she did not much care for her. "Nerthus despises magic and by extension, all mages. I think if it were up to her, she would exterminate the lot of us, but the Emperor has balked at such an extreme action."

"He would even consider it?" Raine said, surprised.

"Yes, actually I think he would. But he knows that mages are a valuable resource in battle, which is the only reason why Nerthus doesn't hold more sway, because in all other things, he values her opinion highly."

"And how does Bristol fit into this?"

"Well, personally I feel that Bristol could have been more vocal in his opposition to Nerthus, but he let her do as she would. She set out on a mission to 'neuter' as many mages as she could."

"How would she do that?"

"She surrounds them with alar silicite."

"Ah," Raine said. Alar silicite was a material known to absorb magical energy, although poorly. One could construct an entire house of stone with it, and it might block ten percent of the power of a moderately strong mage. It was also heavy, which made it unwieldy and difficult to use.

"She's made robes of it, jewelry, created jail cells with it woven into the masonry, even created a wall about the mages' academy."

"But it doesn't work very well," Raine said.

"No, but it's very unpleasant for mages to be around. I've had friends complain of severe headaches, bloody noses, that sort of thing."

"And how does Nerthus treat you?" Raine said a little angrily.

"My magic is not the type that inspires her ire. My gift is in the healing arts, and although she hates all magic, that's the kind she hates the least. And Dagna's position in the court helps."

"So I imagine she's not fond of Black Magic."

"She hates that above all else."

"Hmm," Raine said. "And how does this involve Bristol?"

"As I said, Bristol never agreed with her, but I feel he could have come out more against her. Now he doesn't have a choice."

"How so?"

"Bristol's daughter has begun showing signs of the gift, and she has no control. Nerthus has so gutted the staff of the mages' academy, there are few there who can even stand against her, let alone help. And the girl suffers, for she's tormented by creatures from Nifelheim and fears to even sleep. Her orientation is towards destruction magic, which will spiral into black if not contained."

Raine gave a great sigh. This was a difficult situation.

"And there's another who requires direction."

Raine turned to the wise, ancient voice. "You speak of Isleif's progeny," she said to Y'arren. "Talan felt that as well. The girl is immensely powerful."

"Yes, and she's oblivious to it. That power will attract evil if it's not protected. Isleif wanes in his later years and is not able to protect Skye other than from a distance. And he fears he can't even do that since he was unable to protect Isolde."

Raine thought back to Skye and her companions. "Isleif was wise to send her to the Ha'kan. They will protect her with their lives."

"And the Ha'kan are an extraordinary military power," Y'arren said, "but they're not good with magic. Even their First Scholar, who is skilled, is limited in her ability to help."

Another sigh came forth from Raine and she leaned back, interlacing her fingers behind her head. She glanced over to Elyara.

"Well, I know the perfect person to deal with this because Isleif has a protégé. I'll find her, then travel to the capital to meet up with you in a few weeks. I told the Alfar ambassador that I would meet her there as well, so I can accomplish many things with the same journey."

"Thank you, Raine," Elyara said, "I knew you would be able to help."

"You may not thank me when you see who I bring, but you'll have to trust me," Raine said wryly.

Chapter 9

erthus stood in the courtyard of the Mages' Academy, her arms crossed over her chest. She was large for a human, especially a female, and her heavy imperial armor made her look even larger. She stood next to Bristol, who dwarfed most of his comrades, and he in no way dwarfed her. She had pale blue eyes that were perennially icy in expression and broad, fine features that might have been attractive were it not for that menacing countenance. The lips were full and possibly lovely had they not been pursed in constant disapproval.

They were both watching his daughter, Kelsey, who was unaware of their presence as she listened carefully to her instructor. The two knight commanders had very different expressions on their faces. Bristol struggled as he watched his red-haired daughter. He had wanted her to become a soldier like him, and because she favored him in all ways, looks, coloring, size, and strength, that seemed not just promising, but inevitable. But then she had begun showing signs of magical abilities, abilities she could not control and that caused her great suffering. Bristol's hopes for his daughter were dashed. Even the possibility of battle mage was now far-fetched as the magic in his daughter seemed to control her rather than she, it.

Nerthus, on the other hand, looked at the girl with disdain. This was exactly why she advocated restricting the freedom of mages. Magic was evil, dangerous, and the girl had already injured three people, one seriously, in mishaps. It was her opinion that Bristol's daughter should be restrained, possibly permanently, in a place where her magic would be neutered and she could not harm anyone.

A slender figure was at the gate, and once recognized by the imperial guards, was allowed through. Elyara approached the two of them and Nerthus looked to her with only slightly less disdain. She did not care for mages, and she did not care for elves, an arrogant lot in her opinion. The fact that the elven mage in front of her was both humble and gentle did not alter that opinion in any way.

"Knight Commanders," Elyara said in greeting.

Nerthus gave her little more than a curt nod, but Bristol clasped her hands warmly in his.

"Elyara, thank you so much for your help on this."

"Of course, Bristol, anything that I can do."

"And the mage that was recommended, she's coming?"

"Yes," Elyara said, "she's supposed to be here any moment. It's said she's Isleif's protégé, so she must be extremely talented."

"I hope so," Bristol said, his gaze returning to his daughter. He winced as she lost control of a spell and lit a nearby trellis on fire. Several apprentice mages rushed over with buckets of water, conspicuously prepared for such a possibility. Bristol wondered how many times this had happened before. Nerthus snorted aloud, clearly paralleling his train of thought.

"Well," Elyara said, trying to distract the conversation from the fiasco, "she came with the very highest recommendations as both a mage and a teacher."

Another figure at the gate caught the eye of Nerthus and she turned. Her guards, contrary to all policy and procedure, were simply letting the woman walk right through. And it wasn't as if they didn't see her because they stood gaping as she strolled past them. Elyara also turned, recognizing the figure with half-disbelief, half-delight. Bristol was the last to see her, and he gazed in pure astonishment.

"Surely that can't be who Raine has sent," he said.

The woman had long dark hair and smoldering dark eyes. She wore robes of fine fabric that hugged her form and hid nothing of her curvaceous lines. The neckline plunged nearly to her navel and the full breasts threatened to spill out, prevented perhaps by the magic that swirled in eddies about her. She did not walk; she sauntered in a sultry manner that seemed to leave a trail of scorched earth in her wake. Sensuality permeated every movement, every subtle gesture, every brush of those long, dark eyelashes on the cheeks, and especially in those wicked, laughing eyes.

"Oh no," Nerthus said in disapproval. "No, no, no, no."

Bristol ignored her and stepped forward. "Idonea," he said, still not quite believing she was before him. He had not seen her in twenty years, and she had not aged a day. He, on the other hand, was now a middle-aged man. Elyara looked much the same, but elves were long-lived and that was expected.

"You look wonderful," Bristol said.

Idonea kissed him lightly on the cheek. "A gift from my mother," she said, reminding him she was only half human.

"Ah," he said, remembering, "that's right."

Idonea turned and kissed Elyara on the cheek as well, and Elyara was pleased with the kind gesture for Idonea was not known for kindness.

"And my little elf, how are you?"

"I'm quite wonderful," Elyara said, "and Dagna will be so excited when I tell her you're here."

Nerthus was getting the impression that this mage was well known to the group at hand, but that did not matter to her. She turned to Bristol, speaking as if Idonea were not there.

"This is exactly the kind of influence we're trying to avoid."

Bristol blanched because Idonea had a dangerously volatile temper and skills to match. But that had been the Idonea of twenty years ago, and this one simply turned to the knight commander, angling her profile so that one breast was almost fully revealed, a sardonic look upon her features.

"And what influence is that?" she asked innocently.

Although Nerthus had a reputation for iciness, at least professionally, she also had a near-contradictory reputation for bedding men and women with unrestraint, although sleeping with them once, and only once. And although many wished they could criticize and belittle her in this arena, it was impossible to do so because she was a formidable lover and there were too many accounts to contradict the untruth. If anything, her actions generated bitterness because she had sex with a person but a single time. And although she was forthcoming about it, many still felt discarded or thought they would be an exception, and there were none.

Idonea knew none of this, but she knew people, and could sense desire no matter how deeply buried in ice. Nerthus' eyes were drawn to the breast and were trapped there, unable to break free. With tremendous effort, she raised her gaze back to the laughing dark eyes, her pale skin now flushed with even more anger. She looked down to the onyx star she always wore on a chain about her neck, but the gemstone was not glowing.

Idonea looked to the amulet, recognizing it for what it was. An onyx star was an artifact that could detect magical spells.

"I assure you," Idonea said, entertained, "whatever effect I'm having on you is not due to magic." She cocked her head to one side, "and I must say I find it interesting you use a magical artifact to detect the magic you detest."

Nerthus was livid and both Elyara and Bristol looked away, Elyara to hide her smile and Bristol to hide the enormous pleasure this exchange was giving him.

"Ah, that's just what we need," Nerthus said, "a smart mouth to go with Black Magic."

"And who said anything about Black Magic?" Idonea said, innocent once more.

"I know it when I see it."

"But looks can be deceiving," Idonea said, then promptly contradicted her own words. "Although in this case they're not."

"You will not use Black Magic within the imperial capital," Nerthus commanded.

"Hmm," Idonea said, an ambiguous response that was deeply dissatisfying to the knight commander. Nerthus started to say something, but yet another figure coming through the gate attracted her attention. This one was not stopped, either, and Nerthus thought about thrashing both of the guards on the spot. But she, too, stared at the woman. Where the mage had attracted attention with her earthly sensuality, this one possessed an angelic perfection. Even so it was not her flawless appearance that held Nerthus' attention, but rather the deadly grace with which she moved. Her eyes narrowed and the soldier in her took note: this was a very dangerous, even lethal individual.

Raine smiled a brilliant smile as she approached the group. Bristol gave her a bear-hug, lifting her off her feet, and she pounded him on the shoulders in greeting.

"Am I the only one who's aging here?" he asked.

Raine turned to Elyara and hugged her, then to Idonea, who leaned forward to kiss her on the cheek. Elyara was pleased to see the gesture. Initially, the relationship between Idonea and Raine had been strained and Elyara was happy to see that things had changed. Clearly, however, it was still playfully sarcastic.

"Step-mother," Idonea said in mocking greeting.

"Daughter," Raine said, just as mockingly. The exchange was especially humorous since Idonea and Raine appeared the same age, and Raine perhaps even the younger.

"She's your step-mother?" Nerthus said in disbelief.

"Well, let's just say she's my mother's lover."

Raine grinned at the characterization. She stepped forward and held out her hand, giving a short formal bow.

"My name is Raine, Knight Commander."

Nerthus took the hand, examining the woman before her.

"That doesn't tell me a lot," Nerthus said. She felt a startling surge of lust upon contact with the hand which was surprising because the young woman really wasn't her type. "Half the men and women in Arianthem are named Raine after that poem," she turned to Elyara with obvious distaste, "that your bard wrote."

Bristol had to look away again, covering his mouth. Wouldn't Nerthus be surprised to know she was standing before "the" Raine. They had all agreed there would be no deception, but they had equally agreed there was no sense in revealing information that was not solicited.

Raine reclaimed the hand the knight commander seemed willing to hold onto and turned back to Idonea.

"And how is Isleif?"

"He grows weak," Idonea said, "but the old lecher still finds the strength to grope me at every opportunity."

"Good," Raine said, "so he still has some life in him."

"Don't tell my mother," Idonea said, "but I'm eternally grateful she arranged for me to work with that old wizard. And I owe him more than I can ever repay."

"Well, your secret from your mother is safe with me. And it's likely you're going to have the opportunity to repay Isleif very soon. As much as he likes to fondle you, he had other motives for taking you on as an apprentice years ago." Raine turned her attention to the red-haired student in the courtyard, and Nerthus, to her great displeasure, ceased to exist. "Now, shall we assess your new pupil?" she prompted Idonea, and the two walked into the courtyard. They stood a short distance away and Nerthus thought to tell them to move because they were too close, but then determined if they wished to be foolish, that was their business. Bristol and Elyara also watched with hope and trepidation.

Idonea examined the girl. She was moderately powerful, nothing extraordinary, but she lacked any sort of control. Her brow was wet with concentration, but every spell went awry. She knocked the instructor off-balance with a simple ward spell, then froze a rose bush next to him, causing him to grimace in displeasure. The more she tried, the worse her spell-casting became, and the frustration was evident on her face. It was odd though, the chaos seemed almost directed, as if she were a puppet on strings. Both Raine and Idonea had the same, growing suspicion, which was confirmed when the girl turned toward them, her neck at an awkward angle, the pupils of her eyes slit. For a fraction of a second, her features twisted into a gargoyle-like mask of pure hate.

"Did you see that?" Idonea murmured.

"Oh yes," Raine replied. "And now it knows we're here."

And then in a startling move, the girl sent a blast of fire toward the pair, a pure funnel of flame. And in an even more startling move, the dark-haired mage casually pulled the blue-eyed woman in front of her as they both disappeared into the inferno. All in the courtyard stared in horror at the catastrophe and Nerthus stepped forward in anger and dismay. This is exactly what she had feared would happen and confirmed all her beliefs.

Except when the fire finally stopped, both Raine and Idonea were simply standing there unscathed while the ground around them was blackened and smoking. Idonea gently pushed Raine back to her original position, and Raine moved obediently, as if Idonea's action was both appropriate and expected.

"Thank you," Idonea said casually, her eyes still on the girl.

"You're welcome," Raine said, unmoved by the entire event.

Nerthus whirled on Elyara. "Is Raine also a mage?" she demanded.

"No," Elyara said, "she's the complete opposite."

"What?"

"Raine has no magical ability whatsoever," Elyara explained. "Real fire would burn her, but that was not real fire. It was magical energy that took on the properties of fire. And Raine is immune to magic."

"Immune to magic?" Nerthus said in disbelief. "I've never even heard of such a thing."

Elyara was not going to explain that Raine's unique ability was a consequence of her unique parentage, two very different races that were both highly resistant to magic had produced an offspring that was entirely immune to it.

"What I wouldn't give for such an ability," Nerthus muttered to herself, and Elyara and Bristol cast sideways glances at one another. Thank the gods such a thing was not possible. It was one thing for Raine, who had not a bias or prejudice in her to possess such a gift. It would be disastrous for someone like Nerthus to have such an ability.

Idonea and Raine were still watching Bristol's daughter, who now appeared greatly confused.

"I think it's time for that thing to go," Idonea said.

"I agree," Raine replied, and Idonea lifted her hand. It had a pronounced effect on Bristol's daughter as every limb locked in place and she was unable to move or even balance herself. Indeed, she would have fallen had not Raine stepped to her side and held her upright. Raine felt her entire body grow cold. It was a small one, but it was evil.

Idonea swirled her hand about in a small, graceful circle, as if building momentum, then leaned forward to the empty space in front of her, appeared to grasp something, then made a violent yanking movement backward. A black, filmy cloud was pulled from Kelsey, a cloud that swirled about angrily and sought to solidify itself but could not because of the powerful mage holding it in check. Idonea examined the creature swirling before her, satisfied that she had removed it in its entirety.

"Would you do the honors?" she said.

"With pleasure," Raine replied, and blew out a breath from her lungs. Whenever she was faced with great evil, her body temperature dropped and at times she was able to use the ability as a weapon. She did so now, freezing the murky, ephemeral mass solid. Idonea released it and it fell to the ground, shattering in thousands of pieces which then slowly dissolved, then disappeared.

Kelsey collapsed and Bristol rushed to her side, taking his daughter from Raine and lifting her into his arms.

"What was that thing?"

"It was a Shard Wisp," Idonea said, "a baby Reaper Shard, if you will. Fed enough magical energy, it would eventually grow into a full-grown Reaper."

"By the gods," Bristol said, horrified.

"The good news is that it's gone. Although your daughter needs a great deal of instruction, she'll be much easier to teach now. I'll stay long enough to get her to a place where she's no longer in any danger from such creatures."

"Thank you," Bristol said, almost in tears. Even with his great respect for Raine, he had not dared hope she could help. Yet she and Idonea had done more in five minutes than all the mages in the academy had done in years. He turned to see Nerthus bearing down on them full steam.

"You see, this is just what I'm talking about. If there were no mages, there would be nothing for this creature to feed from."

"There are natural sources of magic these creatures can feed from," Raine said mildly, "and without mages, you couldn't defeat them."

"Then how is it that you fight them?" Nerthus demanded. She still did not believe the whole "immunity to magic" thing.

"Even I use enchanted weapons against such creatures," Raine said, "a regular sword won't do any damage."

"How is it they affect you at all?" Nerthus said, "If you're indeed immune to magic."

"Ah, and there is the crux of the matter. You're confusing magic with evil," Raine said sagely. "Magic doesn't affect me, but evil most definitely does."

The words held a clear admonishment and anger flashed in the knight commander's pale blue eyes. But Raine ignored her and turned back to Idonea.

"Do you have a preference for lodging?"

Idonea opened her mouth to speak, but Nerthus interrupted.

"We can provide lodging here at the academy," she said gruffly, "we're not completely inhospitable."

Not completely, Raine thought to herself, but kept her silence. Idonea found the offer entertaining, sensing there was more to it than mere hospitality.

"Want to keep me close, do you?" Idonea said wickedly, and Nerthus' pale cheeks grew red once more. Raine actually felt sorry for the woman. Idonea grew more like her mother each day, so the poor knight commander didn't stand a chance. Idonea would do with this woman whatever she willed.

"Even so," Raine said, "Fireside is open to you if you wish."

"You know the owners of Fireside?" Nerthus said with skepticism. Fireside was the largest, most luxurious residence in the imperial capital, rivaled only by the imperial palace itself. It was maintained by an enormous staff, but no one was ever seen going in or out. Speculation on the occupants was rampant and it seemed highly unlikely that this mercenary, or whatever she was, could be associated with them.

"I am the owner of Fireside," Raine replied. "True, I spend most of my time in a cave, but I do have residences scattered about Arianthem." She winked at Idonea. "The cave is my favorite, though."

"I wonder why?" Idonea said. Raine had stumbled across her mother in dragon form in the cave over two decades ago, and they had been madly in love ever since.

"Anyway," Raine said, "I have a few things to attend to here in the capital so I'll be here awhile longer. I'll see you later this evening."

Idonea kissed Raine on the cheek once more and Nerthus felt a stirring of emotion she would not admit was jealousy. The dark-haired mage made it worse when she cast those long eyelashes in her direction with a wicked glint in her eye.

"Would you like a goodbye kiss as well?"

Nerthus could not find her voice, merely blushed profusely as the mage sauntered past her, said her goodbyes to Bristol and Elyara, and then disappeared.

Chapter 10

Elyara, Idonea, and Dagna sat around the lounging area in the great hall of Fireside. Raine was stoking the fire in the enormous fireplace. Elyara was recounting the afternoon's events much to the delight of Dagna, who shared Elyara's dislike of Nerthus. Unlike Bristol, Raine had seen Dagna over the years when they spent time in the forest, so she was used to the fact that Dagna now appeared older than all of them. She looked wonderful, however, and Raine was pleased for her and Elyara's happiness. Raine had hoped Bristol would join them, but he wanted to spend the evening with his daughter.

A servant entered and announced guests, which made Raine curious because she was not expecting anyone. She grinned broadly when the two entered, one tall and slender, the other short and stout, and both greatly beloved to her. Dagna clapped her hands together and Elyara squealed with excitement. Even Idonea flashed a brilliant smile.

"Feyden!" Raine exclaimed, "Lorifal!"

Raine pounded Lorifal on the shoulders then lifted him off his feet, no small accomplishment since he was as solid as the stump of an oak tree. And had anyone else, with the possible exception of Feyden, even attempted such an act, it would have ended in a brawl. But the dwarf loved Raine with all his heart and his cheeks went ruddy with happiness. She set him down and turned to Feyden, embracing him, and the taciturn, aloof elf returned the embrace with an enthusiasm that would have stunned all who knew him.

"I can't believe this reunion!" Raine said. She had seen all of them over the years, especially Idonea, but this was the first time they had all been together since the quest. "I only wish Bristol could have come."

"And Gunnar," Elyara added a little sadly.

"And Gunnar," Raine agreed. But she would not allow the sadness to remain. She slid a sideways glance at Lorifal. "Thirsty, my friend?"

"Always," Lorifal said. He glanced about the enormous room. "And I'm guessing by the looks of this place you have quite a stock on hand."

Raine spoke with the servant and brought out something special for each. Elyara received a fine spiced cider with a bit of a bite to it. Dagna took a flagon of honeyed mead, a brew so smooth and light it brought a sigh of pleasure from her. Idonea received a goblet of red wine made from the finest grapes of the Alfar. Feyden took a crisp white wine also made from the grapes of his people, one cooled in the cellars beneath Fireside. And Lorifal downed a glass of anise liqueur, one of his favorites.

"And will you be having your amber sting?" Idonea asked.

"Oh no, no, no," Raine said, "that's not a good idea without your mother around. You know how that affects me." She poured herself a glass of the anise liqueur while refilling Lorifal's. They touched rims, then downed the fiery liquid. It was not as strong as an amber sting, but Raine enjoyed the flush of heat that went through her.

"My sister was quite impressed with you," Feyden said, settling in next to Idonea.

"It was hard to tell," Raine said, "that Alfar reserve is strong in your family."

Feyden laughed, because he was not reserved with Raine at all. "Maeva was pleased to find out you weren't human."

Raine wrinkled her brow. "Why is that?"

"She was very attracted to you, and it bothered her."

"Why would that bother her?" Dagna asked.

Feyden was apologetic. "My sister doesn't like the sons and daughters of men. She's disparaging of them, insulting even." He turned back to Raine. "It's my understanding that the initial meeting with the imperials went very poorly."

"That's unfortunate," Raine said, disappointed. "It's crucial that the Alfar and the empire come to some sort of agreement, even if it's cordial at best."

"I know," Feyden said. "I've pushed her as hard as I can, but she's the eldest in my family, even if by minutes, and I must defer to her." He leaned forward, lowering his voice, although none could overhear. "It's more important than ever that Maeva's opinion be turned. It's little known outside Alfar territory, but it's assumed Maeva will become the next Directorate of the High Council."

"Then she'll be the de facto leader of your people," Raine said.

"Yes," Feyden. "Although the Alfar don't answer to a single leader like the empire or the Ha'kan, the position of Directorate is very powerful."

Raine sighed. "It's interesting then, that she's embarked on this journey as ambassador, a position that seems far beneath her."

Feyden nodded at the astute observation. "I believe she's making up her mind, not just on current matters but future matters as well. It'll be far, far beneath her to engage in diplomatic missions once she's Directorate."

"So, this must succeed," Raine said. "For if she decides the empire is not worth an alliance, she'll soon make that decision for all Alfar."

"Yes," Feyden said quietly.

"And what does she think of the Ha'kan?" Raine asked.

"She's more favorable towards them, although there's work to be done. But the diplomats within the Ha'kan capital find them a gracious and noble people. Not to mention the fact the Alfar are fascinated by their sexual habits."

"Who isn't?" Dagna murmured, and Elyara punched her good-humoredly.

"That's good to know," Raine said. "I'm a better fighter than diplomat, but I'll do what I can."

Feyden was relieved. Although he had been at Raine's side in battle and knew her to be unmatched in skill, he also knew she was the only one, barring a miracle, who could change Maeva's mind.

The knight commander stood in the shadows with two of her soldiers, watching the blue-eyed creature stand before the gates of the elven embassy. She had grilled Bristol on his relationship with her, but he had laughed it off, replying that Raine was "just a friend." She had tried to get information from both Elyara and that bard girlfriend of hers, but they had been equally vague, referring to Raine as a very old friend. And Nerthus was becoming more convinced that the woman was not human, partially because of the graceful, lithe movement that seemed a bit other-worldly, and partially because she was obviously far older than she appeared. Nerthus was beginning to suspect that she was an elven spy, and the fact that she was ushered with great respect and fanfare into the embassy, an embassy that no one but the Alfar was allowed into, confirmed her suspicions. She would have to see if she could get something out of that dark-haired mage.

The Alfar guards ushered Raine through the outer courtyard of the embassy and into the interior hall. Outside the gates, the embassy was imposing but did not appear out-of-the-ordinary. Inside the gates, however, it was spectacular with the elaborate elven architecture the Alfar were famous for. The elven guards examined their guest curiously. No one was allowed inside the embassy, yet this one was being allowed into the personal quarters of the high elven ambassador herself. Maeva limited her sexual trysts to the Alfar, but they surmised perhaps she was making an exception for this one, which was understandable since they, too, felt her magnetic pull. They speculated that the woman was from elven lineage based upon her appearance and grace.

Raine entered the antechamber and Maeva was standing as if waiting for her. She was dressed in the robes of the elven high council and with her stature and demeanor, possessed an arrogant and stately beauty. Raine gave a short bow of respect. Maeva examined her at some length and Raine was patient beneath the inspection.

"It's difficult for me to be around you," Maeva said.

"And why is that?" Raine asked.

Maeva gave a slight smile. "Because I'm not used to wanting something I can't have."

There was no real response to such a statement, so Raine remained silent.

"But," Maeva continued, "as I have no wish to be eaten by a dragon, I'll not press the matter further."

Raine breathed a sigh of relief. That could have been very bad. She was not certain why Maeva had summoned her, but it seemed she wished to toy with her.

"May I ask you a personal question?" Maeva said, settling into a chair that resembled a throne. She gestured to a far less throne-like chair across from her, and Raine sat down with some discomfort. She would have preferred to stand.

"Of course," she said warily. She had a feeling she was not going to enjoy this game.

"Is it true that Arlanians can be forced to orgasm, that they cannot help but climax during sex?"

Raine's jaw clenched and her eyes went to a very pale gray blue, the color of ice. Maeva was angry and willing to take it out on her, although Raine knew she was not the real target of her anger. She kept her tone even when she responded.

"Yes, it's true. My mother's people have no control in that respect."

"And has that ever happened to you?"

"No," Raine said, "I've only been with Talan, so it's never been against my will."

"You've had no lovers other than the dragon?" Maeva asked, fascinated.

"No. I had no lovers before her and wanted no others after."

"Hmm," Maeva said, then thankfully changed the subject. "My brother came in late last night quite joyful and inebriated, so I can only assume he spent the evening with you and that dwarf."

"Yes, both Feyden and Lorifal came to Fireside."

"I should have known you owned Fireside," Maeva said. "I sought to purchase the property at one time and was told it was unavailable, regardless of price."

"You're welcome to stay there any time you wish," Raine said, then regretted her generous nature because it brought the sexual intensity back into those gold-flecked eyes. Raine was not used to being in this position. She was always in control of the situation, but right now she was at a disadvantage because she needed something from Maeva, and Maeva knew it.

"I'm sure that Feyden told you that initial talks with the imperials went poorly."

"Yes," Raine said, "I'm disappointed to hear that. I hope you'll give them another chance."

"I must think about it," Maeva said. "It's my intent to retire to the country for a few weeks. There's an estate on the border between imperial lands and the Alfar republic. I'm going to throw a few parties, invite some of the nobility, get out of the capital for a while."

"That sounds like a good idea," Raine said. "Get away from the politicians, meet some different people."

"Yes, then I'll return to the Dverger to finalize our agreement." Maeva trailed off. Her fingernails were very long, and they made a tapping noise as she drummed her fingers on the armrest of her throne. She turned her wrist to examine the nails, then resumed the drumming motion. Her eyes returned to Raine, almost a caress, lingering with impudence wherever they felt like it. Raine was steadfast beneath the inspection, wondering if Maeva was going to demand she remove her clothing, but when she spoke, her request was far more personal than that.

"I want to see your eyes."

Raine's jaw clenched again and she looked to the floor. This was an invasive request, a mild extortion, a favor demanded in exchange for Maeva's continued effort in the diplomatic process.

"Very well," Raine said. If Maeva wished to play with her, she would play.

Maeva inhaled sharply and drew back, for Raine's eyes were now the most gorgeous color of violet she had ever seen. She understood how the Arlanians had been raped into extinction because the lust those eyes inspired in her was staggering, stealing her breath from her. Legend had described the unearthly beauty of the Arlanians, but those legends paled in comparison to the purple eyes that stared at her. Raine let the natural color remain for a moment, then concentrated and hid it, reverting to the eye color of the Scinterians. Maeva was almost angry at the withdrawal of that which she so desired.

"You may go," Maeva said, dismissing her.

Raine stood. "And I'll see you in a few weeks?"

It was Maeva's turn to clench her jaw, but she would not renege on their unspoken deal. "Yes, I will return to the capital in a few weeks."

"Good," Raine said, then bowed stiffly and took her leave.

She had barely disappeared when Maeva rang the bell calling for her personal servant. The Alfar servant came in and bowed low, sensing his master's tension.

"Bring me something," Maeva said.

"A boy?" Melwen queried, "a girl?"

"It doesn't matter," Maeva snapped. "I just want something small and helpless."

Melwen nodded. The usual it would be.

Chapter 11

The flowerpot exploded, but instead of the usual invectives and groans of displeasure, the dark-haired woman just laughed. Kelsey was not certain what to make of it. She was so used to the unrelenting criticism of her frustrated instructors and the hovering presence of the knight commander, she hardly understood the carefree, offhand manner of this gorgeous woman. And where the other instructors had flinched, even cowered as she attempted her spells, this woman simply stood there, laughingly deflecting anything that went awry. Kelsey started to relax, even got a little bit of a smile on her face. She wasn't even bothered by the considerable audience they had because really, none of them were looking at her. Even the knight commander who was standing back in the shadows was quite fixated on the dark-haired mage.

"That wasn't exactly what I was looking for," Idonea said without a hint of reproach, "but it was a very nice explosion. You just need to relax," she said, patting the girl on the shoulder. "Are you sleeping better?"

"Oh yes," Kelsey said. "The last few nights I've slept better than I have in years. No nightmares."

"Good," Idonea said, "that will only help. Now do you see that bucket of water over there?"

"Yes."

"I want you to freeze the water in it."

A look of doubt appeared on Kelsey's freckled features.

"And I don't want you to freeze the bucket."

Kelsey started to shake her head, but Idonea would have none of it. "Close your eyes. Don't think about freezing it, just picture it done."

This did not sound feasible, but Kelsey obeyed if for no other reason than Idonea was rapidly becoming her idol, overtaking even her father. She closed her eyes, trying to picture the water in the bucket as ice.

"Now open your eyes."

Kelsey's eyes opened. The bucket was not on fire, nothing had exploded, in fact, it looked like nothing at all had happened.

"Go look in the bucket," Idonea said, and Kelsey obeyed. She stared down at the solid block of ice in disbelief.

"I did it," she murmured.

"And you're capable of so much more," Idonea said, joining her. "That creature bedeviled you for so long you lost all confidence. And now you assume that things will go wrong, so they do. You must change that pattern and assume that things will go right, and they will."

"It can't possibly be that easy," Kelsey said.

"You would be surprised," Idonea replied, "some things that seem impossibly complex are actually very simple."

Kelsey followed Idonea's gaze and hid a smile, for the mage was looking directly at the knight commander who was not nearly as well-hidden as she thought. "Now why don't you run off and find that little red-haired boy who can't take his eyes off you?"

"Skipp?" Kelsey said, blushing. "Do you think he likes me?"

"Trust me my dear," Idonea said, her eyes still on the knight commander, "I'm a master of these kind of things."

The explosion was so powerful it shook the walls and so loud that Nerthus was upright from her bed, greatsword in hand, before the walls stopped moving. There was shouting and the sound of running footsteps outside. Nerthus cursed. What had those idiot mages done now? She pushed through her door and onto the second story balcony that looked into the courtyard below. Soldiers were rushing toward a raging fire with buckets of water. She took the stairs in great leaps, landing with surprising agility given her size.

"What happened?" she demanded of a captain who sprinted by her.

"Not certain!" he yelled, "It's in the armory!"

Nerthus frowned. What the hell were the mages doing in the armory? She caught sight of some students coming out of their quarters, frightened but curious.

"Get back in your rooms," she ordered. That was the last thing she needed, more of these fools getting in the way. "I said get back in your rooms!" and they responded, but still peered from their doorways. She stormed over to the edge of the conflagration. It was hot and the sound of the flames was very loud, the fire on the verge of creating its own windstorm.

"What have these idiots done now?" she demanded over the roar.

"They dropped a piece of that black ore we found, the one the Chief Armorer wanted to inspect."

"What?" Nerthus said. "Why were the mages carrying the black ore?"

The commander looked at her blankly. "What? It wasn't the mages. It was the soldiers."

"Not the mages," Idonea said as she sauntered by. She was unaffected by the heat of the inferno and casually waved her right hand toward the fountain in the middle of the courtyard. The water rose up in a towering pillar, sprouted arms and legs, then began walking toward the fire. Steam began to rise from the water being, and when it reached the edge of the burning building, it spread out its arms and appeared to fall forward in self-sacrifice. As it fell, the being broke apart into a giant wave that splashed downward and drowned the fire completely. It was a jaw-dropping display of power, and the soldiers stood there with their buckets in their hands, staring dumbly at the soggy remains. The mages stared from their doorways, stunned, but with the stirrings of pride.

Idonea wiped her hands with satisfaction, then turned on her heel, heading back towards her assigned room. "That was fun," she said.

Nerthus was livid. "I will see you in my chambers."

"What?" Idonea said mildly.

"I will see you in my chambers!" Nerthus repeated, her pale cheeks red with anger, "Now!"

"Very well," Idonea said, but just stood there as Nerthus' anger grew. "I don't know where they are," she said at last, before the knight commander could explode. Nerthus appeared to be chewing on something, so infuriated was she, and she stalked past Idonea. Idonea fell in behind her, noting that it was the first time she had seen the knight commander without her armor on and that really, that square piece of iron did not do her justice. Nerthus stormed up the stairs, her greatsword still in her hand, and Idonea flowed up the stairs behind her. Nerthus kicked the door open, stopping so that Idonea would precede her, and Idonea, unperturbed and serene, did so. Nerthus walked into the room, slammed the door behind her, threw her sword to the side with a great clatter, then stood glaring at the dark-haired mage. Idonea gazed at her expectantly.

"Damn you," Nerthus muttered, then shoved her backward against the wall, pressed her body full against her and buried her tongue in her mouth.

"Mmm," Idonea murmured, her arms snaking upward and over the shoulders where they tangled in the knight commander's hair. It was a small noise of pleasure that somehow communicated how utterly predictable this had been. It was a noise that angered and inflamed the knight commander, and she ripped open Idonea's robe so that her breasts spilled out. Her lips and teeth went to the breasts while she forcefully held Idonea against the wall, and the lips suckled and toyed while the teeth nibbled and bit the nipples that hardened in her mouth. Idonea gasped with pleasure as the mouth went lower and those strong hands ripped the rest of her clothing from her body. The mouth buried itself between her legs while the hands pinned her hips to the wall and the tongue thrust up inside her. She again entangled her fingers in the knight commander's hair, cradling the head that moved with such unrestrained and tortured passion. And Idonea was already coming, her hips moving beneath those incessant lips and that skilled tongue.

But Nerthus was not done with her yet, and she stood and picked Idonea from her feet, carrying her to the bed where she threw her down and again pinned her. She pulled her own robe open so they were flesh-to-flesh and Idonea's hands went about her neck and she kissed her passionately as Nerthus pressed against her, her strong thighs trapping Idonea's leg so that she could create that soft friction and bring herself pleasure. And the knight commander was lost, her hips moving against the voluptuous mage beneath her in near frenzy, her suppressed desire almost violent in its release. And Idonea climaxed again, the feverish movement of the woman on top of her so skillfully implemented it had touched her in exactly the right place again and again until the wetness flowed from her body.

Nerthus collapsed on top of the woman, stunned. Stunned because she had just violated every principle she held dear, and stunned because it had been the most passionate sex in her life. She was breathing harshly, and her heart was pounding, and she could not help but notice how wonderful this woman smelled and tasted. And as exhausted as she was, all she wanted to do was start again. But Idonea patted her on the back, then rolled her off of her. She sat upright, glorious in her nudity, and stretched like a cat.

"Mmm," she said again, "that was fun." She stood up and glanced about. "I'll have to borrow this since you destroyed my clothes." She pulled on Nerthus' robe which was twice her size. "And don't worry, I'll be discreet. Your secret is safe with me." She leaned down and gave Nerthus a peck on the cheek, then headed for the door. "And I'll try and look appropriately chastised tomorrow."

The door closed behind her, and Nerthus just lay there, staring at the door in dumb astonishment.

Bristol was filled with pride. His daughter was demonstrating some basic spells in the courtyard, and although nothing elaborate, they were functioning as intended. Nothing exploded, nothing caught fire, no one was hurt. Even better was the smile on Kelsey's face, a smile shared by her instructors who were slowly but surely incorporating themselves back into her training. Idonea stood at a distance, monitoring the situation. Now that the creature was gone and Kelsey was regaining her confidence, she was quickly improving. Although moderate in power, her determination to refine her skill meant her abilities would rapidly increase. Sometimes willpower was more important than raw talent.

Idonea became aware of a rather large presence at her side and glanced up at the knight commander, who was pretending to watch Kelsey. She appeared uncomfortable and did not look at Idonea when she spoke.

"I would like to apologize for my behavior last night," Nerthus said, "it was inexcusable."

"I forgive you," Idonea said, her lightly mocking tone causing Nerthus to redden. Nerthus hurried to continue.

"And it must not happen again," Nerthus insisted under her breath.

The long dark eyelashes flicked toward her. "Very well," Idonea said as if it were no matter. Just then, Kelsey raised her hands and Idonea did not like what she saw. "Wait," she called out, and left the knight commander standing there.

Nerthus shifted uncertainly, angry, and unsure why she was angry because for once she had received the response she sought. She did not know why she was so irritated. Perhaps it was because her soldiers were acting so unprofessionally and staring at Idonea appreciatively, which elicited a seething glare from her. She felt very out of sorts at the moment.

Idonea corrected Kelsey, adjusting her hand position. Her eyelashes flicked upward and the corner of her mouth twitched as the knight commander stormed from the courtyard.

The temple on the mage academy grounds was small but beautiful. It was late so the temple was dark, lit only by candles. It had altars for various gods and goddesses and little alcoves where worshippers could kneel in prayer. Idonea laid a sprig of lavender on the altar of Sjöfn, admiring the etchings on the raised slab. She was not one of the faithful, but it never hurt to offer up an occasional word of thanks. She heard a noise and turned to see Nerthus behind her. Apparently, the knight commander wore her armor everywhere except to bed.

"Were you afraid I was going to desecrate the temple?" Idonea asked.

"You worship Sjöfn?" Nerthus said in disbelief. It would not seem this one would worship any but Hel.

"She's as good as any other," Idonea said in complete blasphemy. "And do you worship Tyr?"

"Sometimes," Nerthus said stiffly. She did in fact worship the God of War, but Sjöfn, the Goddess of Love, was privately also on her list of favored deities.

"Well," Idonea said serenely, "I will leave you to your worship."

She started past Nerthus, but the woman grabbed her arm. "I—,"

Nerthus started, then stopped.

"Yes?" Idonea said, looking at her with that expectant look that infuriated her.

"Damn you," she said, and lifted Idonea from her feet and onto her back on the altar.

"Oh, you are naughty," Idonea said, getting the words out just before the knight commander plunged her tongue in her mouth. Nerthus' hands were as desperate to undress Idonea as before and she ripped Idonea's gown wide open, causing those creamy breasts to spill out. And now Idonea was completely aroused because she was naked on Sjöfn's altar in the temple of the Imperial Mage's academy with the Emperor's personal knight commander, still in full armor, pinning her on her back. They were completely exposed, and anyone who walked in would be greeted with an astonishing sight, a wicked thought that made Idonea's nipples even harder. Nerthus groaned in tortured desire as her lips went to the nipples, taking as much of the breast into her mouth as she could. Her hand went between the legs and began stroking the softness there, causing those wonderful curvaceous hips to move with such playful and unrestrained abandon. It was maddening to Nerthus, that joyous lack of inhibition, maddening and irresistible. Her mouth went lower to that softness and her own hand slipped beneath her armor to satisfy the need there. And she went to her knees, one hand lightly pinching those pink nipples, her mouth buried in the climax it was bringing forth, and her other hand feverishly bringing her to her own peak. Idonea cried out, then she cried out, muttering several strained profanities that would make Sjöfn herself blush, and then she fell upon the dark-haired mage, her head resting on her stomach.

Idonea stared up at the mural painted on the ceiling and wanted to laugh. The knight commander was proving to be quite a surprise. She knew the woman had some repressed desires, but really, this was delightful. A noise at the temple entrance attracted both of their attentions and Nerthus snatched her from the altar as they both rolled behind it. Nerthus had a panicked expression on her face. There was no way to explain why she was in Sjöfn's temple late at night with a naked mage. Idonea, on the other hand, could barely contain her mirth. Their situation was ridiculous.

"Now this is where magic comes in very handy," Idonea said. She waved her hand, then without hesitation stood upright even though she was fully nude. Nerthus watched in horror as she sauntered across the dais, then down the stairs towards the approaching priest. But the priest did not see the gloriously naked woman who casually walked past him, all he saw was the knight commander peering over Sjöfn's altar at him.

"Is someone there?"

Nerthus started guiltily, then realized she looked like an idiot. She stood upright, straightening her armor.

"Knight Commander," the priest said in surprise.

"Father," Nerthus said stiffly. "I was just kneeling in prayer," she said, red in the face. It was almost the truth.

"I didn't realize you were a supplicant of Sjöfn," the priest said, and Nerthus grew redder because in a way that was even closer to the truth.

"Yes, well," she said uncomfortably, "I have a reputation to maintain, so I keep my worship private."

"I see," the priest said, "then I'll keep your worship private as well."

"Thank you," Nerthus said, then walked down the steps past the baffled priest, then out the door.

Chapter 12

The girl was definitely getting better, Bristol thought. Idonea had pulled off a minor miracle with his daughter. And somehow Idonea had avoided raising the ire of Nerthus which was a far more major miracle in her stay at the capital. The knight commander seemed off-balance right now and many had commented on how distracted she appeared, adding quietly that it was a pleasant change.

In exact contradiction to his thoughts, Nerthus stormed into the courtyard, clearly agitated. She was accompanied by a large contingent of soldiers. Idonea glanced over as Nerthus went directly to Bristol.

"There's a problem in Askel," she said, "we're preparing to ride now."

"What kind of problem?" Bristol asked, concerned. Nerthus was of such high rank it had to be serious for her to go personally.

"Hyr'rok'kin, and they've already killed dozens on the outskirts of the town."

"Hyr'rok'kin?" Bristol exclaimed, "this far into imperial territory?"

"Yes, and not just any Hyr'rok'kin, it's reported there are two of the giant ones."

"Marrow Shards," Bristol breathed out. They were much larger than the regular horde troops of the Hyr'rok'kin. They could be two or three stories high, and massive.

"And something else," Nerthus added, "something I'm not familiar with."

Idonea sidled up to Bristol's side, listening, and Nerthus' pale blue eyes flicked to her in acknowledgment, then back to Bristol. Bristol thought Nerthus would ask her to leave, but surprisingly she did not.

"A farmer described a creature, a smoky black pillar of a monster that faded in and out and screeched horribly. From what the man said, the being can kill with a touch, burning the skin like acid."

Bristol grew very pale and even Idonea's countenance grew serious. Nerthus looked from one to the other. "What is it?"

Bristol deferred to Idonea. "It's a Reaper Shard," she said quietly, "a very deadly and evil creature. It lives half in this world, half in the Underworld, and fades between the two."

"Is Raine still here?" Bristol asked her urgently.

"No," Idonea said. "She escorted Elyara back to Y'arren and won't return for a few days."

"Damn," Bristol muttered. Nerthus was growing angry at the conversation. Imperial troops did not need help from some mercenary.

"You must go," Bristol said to Idonea.

"No," Nerthus said, cutting him off, and Bristol turned to her angrily.

"You can't defeat that thing without magic!"

But Idonea sensed Nerthus' reluctance was for once not due to her disdain for magic.

"Don't want me in harm's way?" she said, slightly mocking, slightly teasing. "Trust me, I'm far more dangerous than I look."

"I have no doubt about that," Nerthus said, "in fact I've seen it firsthand." Bristol looked from one to the other, for it was a very curious conversation. Nerthus seemed at war with herself, then finally, to Bristol's astonishment, relented.

"Fine. You'll accompany the force, but you'll not endanger yourself."

"Hmm," Idonea said. "No promises on that one, but I'll do my best."

The two Marrow Shards were indeed enormous, and Nerthus, who faced most enemies without a trace of fear felt a shock of alarm upon seeing them. They were in a valley below them, surrounded by a Shard horde, and the group as a whole was feeding on a herd of mutilated cattle. Bristol, too, was afraid, but his was an old fear based on experience. He desperately wished Raine was here, who would take down these two monstrosities single-handedly, laughing the whole time. But he took comfort in Idonea's presence because her skill had aided their quest years ago, and now that skill had increased exponentially.

Idonea gazed down at the horde, coolly assessing the monsters. She was not greatly concerned with the gigantic beasts; although difficult, they could be dealt with by brute force. No, what she was looking for was not yet here. She held back while Nerthus led the charge down the hill, and the imperial troops collided with the Hyr'rok'kin horde in a spray of blood. It was a more pitched battle than Idonea was used to because generally Raine was with her when she battled Hyr'rok'kin, and although the imperial troops were brave, she would take Raine over an entire regiment. Nerthus was impressive, however, swinging her greatsword with deadly force and accuracy, and although the Marrow Shards were not going down, at least they were being chipped away at piece by piece.

Idonea let her horse pick its way through the carnage. It was near, she could smell it. And it could sense her, circling warily, hungrily, its excitement growing. And finally, at last, she could feel it forming, solidifying right behind her, seeking to catch her unaware.

"By the gods, what is that?" Nerthus said, and Bristol turned at her tone. His heart leaped up into his throat as the Reaper Shard materialized behind Idonea. It was hideous, terrifying, and it lashed out with a smoky black limb, right toward the dark-haired mage.

"Idonea!" Bristol screamed, but Idonea had already sensed the attack and leaned back just enough so the limb shot by her. It instead impaled an imperial soldier, sliding through his torso like a hot poker through wax and killing him instantly. The limb whipped back as if to make another strike, but oddly, its prey was moving closer. The monstrosity grinned, revealing a mouth full of rows and rows of fang-like teeth that went down the length of its endless gullet. It reared back, shrieking an awful scream that caused soldiers and Hyr'rok'kin alike to tremble in fear and cover their ears, then dove forward, seeking to consume the body of its prey in one gulp.

But it would not complete its lunge, for Idonea did little more than hold up her hand to touch the creature, and it froze into a solid block of ice. The ice spread outward from the creature, crackling like a small, fast-moving glacier, and overtook the Hyr'rok'kin Shards one-by-one in startling fashion. They froze in place, looking like hideous malformed statues, even their expressions locked. The Marrow Shards looked on dumbly as the ice formed about their feet, hardened in place, then began snaking up their legs. They struggled and tried to pull free as the pain from the intense cold took hold, but it was to no avail. They roared in rage as it encased their torsos, then their arms, then traveled up to their heads until they were frozen solid and at last silent. Within seconds, the entire Hyr'rok'kin force was encased in solid ice.

Nerthus struggled to pull her sword free, which had been impaled in a Hyr'rok'kin who was now frozen. It came loose, knocking the creature's frozen arm off as it did so. She looked at Idonea with awe and a little fear.

"They will eventually thaw out," Idonea said drily, "I suggest you hit them."

And so Nerthus did, with a great cry she swung her sword and shattered the frozen creature in front of her in a thousand pieces. The other soldiers also let loose cries and began swinging at their frozen enemy. And a group of them began chopping at the legs of the Marrow Shards until they were felled like great trees, falling in slow motion and shattering like glass when they struck the ground. All the soldiers were breathing hard when at last no more Hyr'rok'kin stood. Bristol walked to Idonea's side, staring at her in wonder.

"Idonea, I—," he trailed off, having no words. She had been strong years before, but now her power was incredible.

"I've been practicing," she said, and turned to Nerthus as the knight commander approached. A wave of dizziness overtook her, and she swayed, appearing as if she might collapse. Instantly, Nerthus was at her side and swept her from her feet.

"You're injured," she said, concerned.

Idonea was amused at the protective, even possessive action. "No," she said, "I'm just tired. That was difficult even for me."

"I'll get you someplace safe," Nerthus promised. She reddened slightly when she realized her entire troop was gaping at the sight of their formidable knight commander, who hated mages, holding one ever-so-gently in her arms.

"Make certain they're all dead," she said to Bristol gruffly, who normally would have been angered by the fact his equal was giving him orders but right now was so perplexed by her uncharacteristic actions he just obeyed.

"Very well," he said, and Nerthus stalked off, still carrying Idonea. She assisted the dark-haired woman onto her own horse, then climbed up behind her, supporting Idonea so she could lean back against her. And that sight, somehow, was more astonishing to the imperial soldiers than the manifestation and defeat of the Reaper Shard.

Idonea was more tired than she would admit and fell asleep against the knight commander. Nerthus was concerned for her, wishing they were closer to the capital so the woman could rest. There was a small chapel up ahead, one that was closed for repairs, and Nerthus thought it might be a good place for a brief respite. She would not admit it, but it was also somewhere she could be with the dark-haired mage alone, away from prying eyes and rampant speculation.

She dismounted and lifted the mage from the horse, carrying her inside. She kicked the door shut behind her and looked about in the dim light. It was under repair, but still cared for, and there was a small side rectory where presumably a priest or priestess lived. It was empty now, and Nerthus laid Idonea down on the small bed. She cracked the window so a small breeze came through but closed the curtains so Idonea could sleep. She then began to do undo the straps on her armor.

"Going to rape me in my sleep, are you?" Idonea murmured.

Nerthus struggled with the straps. "Apparently not as I can't seem to get out of my armor." She generally had the assistance of her servants. "Don't you have some sort of spell for this sort of thing?" Nerthus said.

"Ah yes," Idonea replied, "the 'make-you-naked' spell. I'm still working on that one."

"Seems like it would be useful," Nerthus muttered.

"'Tis a good thing you're not a mage," Idonea said sleepily.

"Hmmph," Nerthus said. The straps finally came loose, and she set the heavy armor aside. She did not feel the weight when it was upon her, but she felt very light once it was off. She removed her gauntlets and greaves as well.

"That's better," Idonea said, examining the full figure with appreciation. "As much as I enjoyed our little romp in the temple, I missed seeing those magnificent breasts."

Nerthus reddened a little. She had always been proud of her height, but a little self-conscious of her very large breasts. She had despised the stares of men when she had been younger, the eyes that could never quite make it to her face, but now the open, appreciative stare of this woman filled her with warmth.

"You'd better get into this bed or I'll start pleasuring myself in front of you."

"I might like that," Nerthus said, climbing into the bed behind her, "but I have a feeling you're too tired."

"To have sex?" Idonea said.

"No," Nerthus said, sliding her hand across Idonea's hip and down between her legs. "To do it yourself."

"Mmm," Idonea said, pressing her back against those breasts as the hand gently stroked her. She was not certain she could climax, so great was her fatigue, but the gentleness of this seduction, a stark contrast to their previous couplings, was perfect for her current mood. And as the knight commander nibbled on her neck and buried her face in her hair, Idonea's hips responded to that gentle stroking and she found herself coming as the woman held her tightly to her. And it was barely over when Idonea felt herself falling into a deep, peaceful, exhausted sleep.

The slice on her arm woke her. It was not greatly painful, little more than a prick; it was just that it was unexpected. She was groggy and was having a hard time focusing, so she could barely make out the tiny vial held beneath the wound in her arm, collecting drops of her blood.

Idonea began struggling wildly but Nerthus was very large and easily controlled her. Under normal circumstances, Idonea would have blasted her with some sort of magic, but she was still exhausted from her battle with the Hyr'rok'kin.

"Stop it," Nerthus said, but Idonea was furious.

"How dare you!" she spit out. She tried to snatch the vial from Nerthus, but Nerthus held it away from her. Idonea stared at the tiny glass container in fury. It was whispered that the empire took samples from their mages and had secured them in a cave somewhere. It was a paranoid, preventative measure because it was rumored that a mage could be tracked with their own blood. Idonea was furious because it was not just a rumor; it was true. Raine would slit this woman's throat, and her mother, her mother would do far worse.

"Are you going to put it in your cave with the rest of your vials? The empire's pathetic attempt to subjugate what they don't understand?"

"I'm not going to put it in a cave," Nerthus said calmly, still controlling Idonea by straddling her. She carefully threaded a gold chain through the catch in the vial, then put the necklace about her neck. Idonea stopped struggling, staring at the vial that settled in the valley between those two great breasts. She narrowed her eyes, suspicious, but less angry.

"What are you doing?"

Nerthus looked down at her, her jaw working. She was having a very difficult time saying what she needed to say. "I just want to be able to find you if you need me."

Idonea wasn't certain if this was splendidly romantic or frighteningly psychotic. It actually was both, but because of the wildness of her nature, she found it arousing.

"You could have asked," Idonea said chidingly.

"I'm sure that would have ended with me being transformed into a toad or something of the like."

"That's still a possibility."

Nerthus stretched out upon her. "Then I'll have to make certain you're too tired to do it anytime, soon."

"Won't your men be missing you?" Idonea said sarcastically.

"Shut up," Nerthus said, and kissed her so she would.

The silence in the courtyard was too much. Training was proceeding as normal, but there was little conversation beyond the clanking of shields and swords. Nerthus looked about, and none would meet her eye. Her men had been bouncing about uncertainly ever since she returned. She knew they would talk about what happened at the battlefield, and the fact that she had returned over a day later with Idonea on the back of her horse undoubtedly fueled rampant talk. But she could not let it affect troop morale, so she was going to have to address it head-on.

"Harald, come here."

The junior soldier started, then obeyed. Nerthus picked him because she knew him to be honest and brave enough to speak his mind, even if it got him in trouble. She started to speak, then clamped her jaw shut. He stood there dutifully while she gathered her thoughts.

"The men think me a hypocrite, don't they?" she said at last.

"What?" Harald said, startled. "No, no, that's not what they think at all."

"Well, then what—," she waved her hand about the odd behavior in the yard, "what's this all about?"

"Permission to speak frankly, Knight Commander?"

"Yes," Nerthus said, vexed, "please do."

"Frankly," Harald said, repeating himself because he was nervous. He gathered his courage and then just spit it out. "Frankly, the men are just in awe that you're bedding that mage."

"What?" Nerthus said, startled.

Harald clearly could not stop himself. "I mean, by the gods, commander, she must be a hellcat!"

Nerthus stared at him dumbly. "You have no idea," she murmured, then caught herself. "That'll be enough, soldier. Thank you."

She watched him go, then turned back to her men. She had interpreted their demeanor in light of her own guilty conscience, but now that she looked closer, they did indeed cast admiring, even envious glances in her direction. It gave her an odd sense of warmth, and for once, she stood upright with no thought of trying to hide her very buxom figure.

Chapter 13

The cool air of the countryside brought Maeva a small degree of relief. She found the sons and daughters of men insufferable, and the imperial cities were absent all beauty and grace to which the Alfar were so accustomed. Her disdain for humankind had only grown with her preliminary meetings with the imperials. She found them coarse and vulgar, lacking in refinement and subtlety. The "Emperor," as he styled himself had a bloodline that stretched back a few decades, its beginnings drenched in blood and conquest. Her bloodline, on the other hand, stretched back millennia and had been founded in nobility and merit. Despite her brother's continual prompting, Maeva was tempted to leave the imperials to the Hyr'rok'kin. She was far more disposed toward the Ha'kan, and with the upcoming finalization of the treaty with the Dverger, she was not certain if the Alfar needed the imperials. Perhaps it would be better to sacrifice them since imperial territory bordered the Empty Land and they would bear the brunt of the Hyr'rok'kin invasion.

Still, she thought, glancing at her guest list, there were a few amongst the imperials she held in esteem. Maeva was pleased to see that the Lady Jorden would be attending her soiree. Jorden came from an impeccable lineage going back much farther than the upstart of an emperor, but that was not what made her company so welcome. Jorden had a secret that few but Maeva knew, that she had an alter-ego as "Lagmann," the shadowy and allegedly male head of the Guild of Thieves. To Maeva's mind, Jorden was marvelously immoral with a wicked sense of humor. She had also indirectly played a part in Maeva's rise to power as Maeva had criticized the security of the empire in front of the Alfar High Council, and when challenged on her views, was able to produce the Emperor's personal scepter as proof. The Guild of Thieves was apolitical and went wherever the business was good, and business with the Alfar was always good.

Maeva was also greatly pleased that the Lord and Lady Storr had responded. The couple were notoriously reclusive and had not been seen in years. In fact, she had sent the invitation as a courtesy with no expectation of response. Rumors swirled about the couple, of how lovely the Lady Storr was, and how devastatingly handsome his lordship was, but no one could personally vouch for this. Maeva knew that numerous invitations to the imperial court had been politely declined over time, and that this current acceptance was a monumental coup.

It was not merely a social coup, however, but one with vast political implications as well. The House of Storr were the largest private landholders in all of Arianthem, possessing a vast swathe of land that bordered Alfar territory. "Bordered" was perhaps an underestimation in terms; it was the border. And because the Storrs were mild-mannered and generous, there were no disputes if Alfar hunters wandered into their hold, no attempt to control or restrict the roadways, no attempt to eject the Alfar farmers who settled precariously near the perimeter, even those that sprawled into the fecund valley that was undisputedly owned by the Storrs. Had the land been owned by a more aggressive holder, it is likely the Alfar and the empire would already have been at war.

Yes, this was all turning out far better than she had hoped, Maeva thought. Her soiree was transitioning from something she thought to endure to something she might actually enjoy. She stood, changing her mind about her choice of clothing for dinnerware, and went to dress in her most impressive finery.

The steward climbed down from the carriage and approached the gate with a degree of trepidation. The guards at the gate were fearsome in their gleaming elven armor, their expressions impassive and intimidating. The elven overseer at the gate was no less intimidating, and although not dressed in armor, was dressed in regalia just as daunting. Melwen glanced to the carriage, then to the approaching steward, his sharp features neutral. Appearances were irrelevant. All that mattered was whether or not the guests were on the list in front of him. This man was obviously a servant, a high-level one, but clearly not of the nobility. His kindly expression was tinged with nervousness and his florid complexion indicated he was far too fond of drink. In any other circumstances, Melwen would dismiss the man, but tonight, all that mattered was whether his name was on the paper in his hands.

It was a good thing that Melwen had not dismissed him.

"I'm here to present the House of Storr," Oleif said.

Melwen's eyes came up from the paper, an almost imperceptible movement that for him was the equivalent of his head jerking upright. His eyes flicked to the carriage. "Of course," he said, "the House of Storr is most warmly welcomed."

Oleif turned back and motioned to the carriage, and another servant opened the carriage door. A figure stepped carefully down the steps, assisted gently by the other attendant. Melwen simply stared.

It was a young woman, little more than a girl, a petite, dazzling little thing with jet-black hair and startling blue eyes. Her skin was fair, her cheeks tinged with the blush of youth, her lips an exquisite shade of rose. She looked about shyly, her demeanor demure, and in that instant, Melwen knew that everything about the evening had just changed.

"Where are the Lord and Lady Storr?"

Oleif cleared his throat uncomfortably. "The Lord and Lady passed two years ago, within days of one another. This is their daughter, Kiren."

Melwen stared some more. How was it possible that this monumental news was unknown to both the Alfar and the empire? He knew for a fact the imperials were unaware of the passing of the Storrs, because the Alfar spy network was such that if the imperials knew, the Alfar knew. No, of this he was sure, no one from either nation knew that the torch had passed in the House of Storr, and more significantly, that it had passed into the hands of this infant.

Unlike all previous protocol in which he had waited for the guests to approach, Melwen walked to the stopped carriage. He looked down at the young woman, then bowed from the waist with respect.

"The Alfar welcome the House of Storr," Melwen said formally.

"Thank you," Kiren said, her speech graceful and refined, "I'm honored by the invitation."

Melwen motioned to his assistant to escort the girl inside and watched the young lady flow through the gates. Yes, he thought to himself, everything about the evening had just changed.

Glassware tinkled above light laughter and low conversation. Maeva moved among the guests, the consummate hostess, mentally assessing and cataloguing every individual present. She had a checklist in her mind, a wealth of information available on every person present. There was the Duke, something of a blow-hard with a severe gambling problem, but a man not particularly fond of the Emperor. His wife, the Duchess, had a penchant for men half her age and after a few drinks would likely begin propositioning the elven servants. Maeva had given Melwen explicit instructions to provide such an encounter for her, then to discreetly "discover" it, thereby providing the potential for some future extortion. There was the priest from Trygg, a man from a very wealthy family who outwardly decried magic but secretly practiced the black arts himself. And there was the Baron and Baroness, an utterly staid and boring couple who were rumored to enjoy the company of farm animals. Maeva did not know if that was true, but her opinion of the imperials was so low she decided to believe it unless provided proof to the contrary.

She was pleased, however, to meet a pair of laughing, blue-green eyes. The Lady Jorden was making her way through the throng of people, accompanied by a rakishly good-looking woman. Her companion was well-dressed and appeared at ease in the setting, although to Maeva's practiced eye it was the ease of someone who was good at role-play, not the ease of someone used to a formal event. It was likely that the rogue would be just as at ease on the docks somewhere in the seedy part of town, and judging by the way she moved and the way her eyes assessed the wealth around her, Maeva guessed that this was a masterful thief.

"Maeva," Jorden said, approaching the elven dignitary and extending her hands. Both women had a reputation for icy reserve in public, and in that way that icy, powerful women do, they pecked one another on the cheek. But Maeva knew that the Lady Jorden had a volcano beneath her glacial exterior, and because Jorden's intelligence network was only slightly less comprehensive than the Alfar's, she knew Maeva possessed the same.

"Lady Jorden, thank you for accepting my invitation."

"I wouldn't miss it for the world," Jorden replied. She gestured to her companion, "and this is Syn."

The name caught Maeva's attention and her eyes flicked back to Jorden. When the Emperor's scepter had been stolen, the thief had written "Sin" on the sleeping monarch's forehead. Most thought it was an indictment or political statement, but Maeva had the sudden thought it might have been nothing more than a prank by the rake in front of her.

Syn extended her hand and Maeva took it. A circular bruise about the woman's wrist caught her eye and for a brief moment she held the appendage, turning the wrist slightly so she could examine the injury. Her eyes missed nothing, and they moved to the other wrist which bore a matching mark. A smile twitched about her lips, partially because her intelligence on the Lady Jorden's predilections as a dominatrix was accurate, and partially because those predilections made her like the Lady Jorden even more. Jorden was entertained by the successful sleuthing on Maeva's part, and Syn merely sighed.

"Thank you for your hospitality," Syn said politely.

Maeva leaned forward. "You're not going to steal anything while you're here, are you?" she said in a conspiratorial whisper.

"I don't know," Syn said, briefly dropping her act, "if that Duke keeps ogling Jorden's breasts, I might fleece him and his wife."

"Syn!" Jorden said, scolding, "You promised."

Syn sighed again. "Very well, I'll behave."

Maeva laughed and Jorden and her lover moved on. Really, those two had been the highlight thus far and the rest of the guests had merely confirmed her very low opinion of imperials and humankind in general. She glanced about the room, a little irritated over the fact that Melwen was hovering at her elbow. She did not need anything right now so was not certain why he was standing there. Her gaze continued to sweep the crowd. A nondescript fellow with gray hair stood uncomfortably in the corner and Maeva's eyes narrowed. The man looked like a servant. Worse, he seemed to be guarding the corner of the room. Maeva leaned to Melwen, intending to order him to have the man removed when her new vantage point revealed what was behind him. She stopped.

Melwen had been waiting for Maeva's discovery and now waited patiently for the question he knew was coming.

"Who is that?" Maeva murmured, her entire attention now on the corner.

"Her name is Kiren," Melwen said, "she is here representing the House of Storr."

Maeva cast him a sharp glance. "Where are the Lord and Lady Storr?"

"Apparently," Melwen said, his calmness merely amplifying the monumental failure of their intelligence agents, "they've been dead for two years. That's their daughter."

Maeva's eyes returned to the young woman in the corner. She should have cared far more about the political ramifications of the woman's identity, but at the moment, she cared not at all. The woman-child, for she was little more than that, was exactly everything Maeva desired. She was small, petite even. She looked around shyly and was oblivious to the admiring glances cast her way. She was stunningly beautiful with a striking combination of raven-black hair and sapphire-blue eyes.

"Who is the man with her?"

Melwen was prepared with answers because he had been engaged in non-stop inquiry since the Storr carriage had arrived.

"He has acted as the young woman's guardian, a steward of sorts although it doesn't appear he has any legal standing."

"He likes his drink," Maeva commented, identifying the man's weakness with pin-point accuracy.

"Yes."

"You will see that he receives excellent service," Maeva said.

"Of course," Melwen replied. He had already given that directive, for he knew Maeva well. And it was not his position to judge or advise, it was simply his job to obey. And as he watched Maeva move about the room, her eyes magnetically returning to the corner, he knew that his judgment or advice would have mattered little, for his mistress would do exactly as she wanted regardless of consequences, even if it brought the empire and the Alfar to the brink of war.

Kiren felt flushed. The party was all very exciting, but it was beginning to wear on her. She spent so much time alone it was overwhelming to be around so many people. Oleif had informed her in a slurring tone that he needed to relieve himself, and he had disappeared. She was a little worried about him because he did not handle his alcohol well, and he had been drinking since he arrived. Still, she thought he would be fine if she stepped out for a breath of fresh air.

She went through a set of double doors that she thought led to the entryway, but about halfway down the hall she slowed, realizing she was heading further into the mansion. She turned about and nearly ran into a beautiful elven woman with almond shaped eyes that gazed at her intently.

"Pardon me," Kiren stammered.

"Are you lost?" Maeva asked.

"No, I mean yes. I'm sorry. I just thought to get a breath of fresh air."

"I see," Maeva said, "are you having a good time? It would distress me to know you're not enjoying my party."

"I—" Kiren started, then stopped. "Your party? You mean you're—?"

Maeva laughed. "You're precious," she said. "Half the sycophants in Arianthem are here to lick my boots, and you don't even know who I am."

Kiren blushed and Maeva found it utterly charming. A coil of desire twisted in her torso. Her eyes drifted to a decanter on a nearby shelf.

"Would you like a drink?"

Kiren looked at the decanter uncertainly. "I've never really had spirits."

"It could be our secret," Maeva prompted.

The attention of the beautiful elven woman made Kiren feel very warm. "Very well," she said, curious to try the drink.

Maeva poured them both a glassful, but merely pretended to drink from hers as she watched Kiren closely. The young woman took a cautious drink, but that would be sufficient. It was a very special concoction, one of Maeva's favorites. Just enough to dull the senses with no loss of sensation anywhere else. She was not used to seducing humans because they so rarely attracted her. With the Alfar it was simple. Her position was so exalted that submission was the only option, and in truth, even that was unnecessary as her magnetism was such that nearly all yielded to her willingly. Unfortunately for her young lovers, she always quickly grew tired of them.

Kiren swayed and Maeva caught her, taking the drink from her hand before she could spill it. Maeva looked down the hallway to the double doors where Melwen was observing the scene. The two guards that flanked him took their positions outside the doorway as he slowly closed the double doors, leaving the young woman to her fate.

"I'm sorry," Kiren stammered, "I'm not used to spirits."

"That's all right," Maeva said, guiding her to a nearby bench, "you just need to sit down for a minute."

Kiren sat down and Maeva sat down next to her, still supporting her. And when Kiren swayed toward her again, the feel of that small, warm body pressed up against hers was too much. She took Kiren's chin in her hand, tilted her face upwards, and began to softly kiss her. Kiren jumped a little but did not pull away, startled but not afraid. She wasn't really certain what was happening, and she felt very befuddled right now, but the soft lips on her own were very pleasant. And when the tongue gently probed then parted her lips, she made a small inadvertent noise. The tongue went deeper, and she tentatively touched it with her own.

The touch of the tongue was like a shock of lightning to Maeva and she fought to control her own lust. Although demanding and generally focused on her own satisfaction, she usually sought to bring pleasure to her conquest if for no other reason than it intensified her own. But this little one's hesitant response was more of an aphrodisiac than the most powerful potions the elven mages could create, and her arousal was peaking quickly. She stood and lifted the young woman into her arms, then flowed down the hallway with her captive.

"I think you'll feel better if you lie down," Maeva said.

Kiren felt a little dizzy and was having a hard time thinking clearly. She couldn't even remember where she was right now. All she knew is that it was a strange and wondrous feeling to be pressed against this woman's breasts and she turned her head so that she could look at them. Maeva observed the action and felt the wetness between her legs as her body responded. If she were not certain this girl was an innocent, she would suspect that she was the one being seduced.

She carried the young woman past the elven guards who stood outside her personal chambers. They left the door open, resuming their posts impassively. It was not unusual for elven nobility to have sex right in front of their servants. Servants were expected to be nameless, faceless, without expression, seeing nothing, hearing nothing, knowing nothing. The caste structure within elven society was so extreme that servants who violated this unspoken understanding could be killed without question.

Maeva carried Kiren to the enormous, four-poster bed and laid her down. Kiren looked about her in consternation, trying to figure out where she was. Maeva stood back for a moment, taking in the sight of that beautiful little thing in her bed, but her passion wouldn't wait much longer. She reached down and skillfully undid the buttons on Kiren's blouse, pulled the fabric apart, then set her lips upon what lie beneath.

Kiren exhaled sharply and made a small noise as the mouth covered her breast. She had thought the kiss on her mouth was pleasant but this one was astonishing. It made her feel things everywhere, even the parts of her that weren't being touched. She especially felt it between her legs, an area which was suddenly alive with warmth and wetness and arched upward with some unexplained need.

Maeva watched the reaction with incredulous pleasure. She had no doubt of her skill as a lover, but such unrestrained passion was unusual for the Alfar and from what she had seen, was not typical of humans, either. It was apparent the young woman had no idea what she was doing or what was happening, but that she was responding in a marvelously instinctive manner. Maeva wanted to satisfy that instinctive response and pulled the girl's skirt up and thrust her fingers inside her. She felt the resistance that confirmed this was her first time and Maeva issued a low groan of pleasure and put her mouth fully upon the throbbing center of that soft, dark hair. She brought Kiren quickly to climax, those little hips twisting beneath her onslaught as those blue eyes closed in ecstasy and her body trembled with the release of pleasure.

The warm dampness between Kiren's legs would help with what would come next but it was not sufficient, and Maeva dipped her fingers into the bowl of oil on her nightstand. She caressed Kiren, carefully preparing her for the next act, for Maeva had determined to take the girl's innocence the minute she had felt it. Maeva felt almost possessed as she pulled the length of her body on top of the slender frame. Kiren stared up at her, a little confused, a little dazed, and completely overwhelmed by the depth of the experience. But she looked to Maeva with trust, a trust that Maeva was about to completely violate.

"Like many of the Alfar, I'm capable of mild shape-shifting," Maeva whispered to her. "Do you know what that means?"

"No," Kiren said uncertainly.

"Then let me show you," Maeva said, then thrust into her. Kiren arched upward in pain, clinging to Maeva, an act of compliance that drove her mad. She did not know why she was acting with such complete lack of control. She had taken the virginity of many, both male and female; it was her prerogative by her position and authority, and most considered it an honor. But she was normally far more gentle about it. Instead, right now she was driving into this young woman with no semblance of restraint. She knew she was causing her pain and did not care. Her desire was overpowering all sense of reason or decorum. And then, astonishingly, despite the pain and discomfort, those little hips began to move beneath her, then to thrust upward to meet each downward drive. Kiren began to respond to Maeva's movement almost as if she could not help it, as if pleasure would be wrung from her body even if it was against her will.

As completely out of control as she was, Maeva held her pleasure just long enough to make certain the young woman was again climaxing, then let loose her own, forceful orgasm on top of her. Wave after wave of violent pleasure shook her until she had nothing left and she fell upon the girl in total numbness.

After her breathing returned to normal, Maeva lifted her face which had been buried in that jet-black hair. The blue eyes stared at her uncertainly. There was no anger or recrimination in them, only a gentle confusion that made Maeva want to put her in a golden cage for the rest of her life, a cage that would both keep her safe and keep her from all others. It was a startling and fierce emotion, and one that Maeva had never felt before.

Maeva leaned over to the nightstand, this time removing a sponge that she dabbed in the small bowl. She pressed the sponge to Kiren's lips.

"Here," she said quietly, "take this."

And with that curious compliance that was not submission or weakness, rather just a deep and placid passivity, Kiren obeyed, wincing slightly at the bitter taste. And she said not a word as her eyes grew heavy as a result of the drug, but instead just completely relaxed as she went to sleep.

The elven guards stood outside the doorway, both staring ahead at nothing. They spoke not a word and moved not an inch during the entire sexual escapade. The only sign that either knew anything of the events happening just behind them was the bead of sweat that ran down the temple of the guard on the right, even though it was the middle of winter and icily cold.

Melwen nodded to the guards who stood outside the door to Maeva's chambers. She had not returned to the party, which was a trace unusual. He had expected her to finish her conquest, as was her routine, then return to the soiree. But she had not done so. It was a simple enough matter for him to make excuses for her, and all the guests continued to enjoy themselves. No one questioned anything, except perhaps the Lady Jorden, who commented upon her departure how unfortunate it was that both the ambassador and the daughter of the House of Storr had both taken ill at the same time.

Maeva sat at her desk, a look of deep contemplation on her face as she gazed at the figure in the rumpled sheets. Her expression filled Melwen with a deep sense of foreboding, and he spoke with uncharacteristic frankness.

"That is usually the look on your face prior to the seduction. Never after."

"I like this one," Maeva said, "I think I may keep her for a while."

Melwen was flabbergasted by the boldness of the response, for that was audacious even for Maeva. Not only had she just seduced, or, he thought, glancing at the condition of the bed, perhaps even raped, the daughter of one of the most prestigious houses in all the empire, now she was intending to take the young woman captive.

"And so, you've determined to go to war with the imperials?"

Maeva ignored the thinly veiled implication. "I hardly think that will be the outcome," she replied. "From what you've said, they didn't know of her existence until last night."

"Yes, but word will travel quickly to the imperial capital, if it hasn't reached there already. And they will learn that the titular heir of the largest territory in all of Arianthem was last seen in your company."

"Hmm, yes," Maeva said, "and such a young, vulnerable, ally of the Alfar should be protected, don't you think? There are many in the empire who would take advantage of her."

Melwen carefully controlled his tone. The one who would most take advantage of her already had and was sitting in this room. But Maeva liked the direction of this narrative and continued.

"In fact, I think it highly appropriate that I take her into my protective custody since she was clearly harmed last night as a result of her 'guardian's' incompetence and inattention."

The audacity of this last statement was enough to silence Melwen. The fact that she had orchestrated Oleif's inattention then inflicted the harm on the young lady herself seemed irrelevant to Maeva.

"In fact," Maeva continued. "I'll speak with the guardian myself, to impress upon him how seriously the Alfar take his breach of responsibility. In the meantime, have my personal physician examine her to make certain she's not injured, then have her bathed. She'll not awaken anytime soon."

"Oh, and by the way," Maeva said, pausing on her way to the door. "How old is she?"

Melwen carefully controlled his expression. Really, that was a question most would have asked before. "If she were Alfar, she would be too young."

Maeva gazed at him expectantly. That meant nothing, for the Alfar were much longer-lived than humankind, and their development was adjusted accordingly.

"But by the very loose and crude standards of the empire, she is of age."

"Good," Maeva said over her shoulder, "I'd hate to violate their customs."

Oleif sat in the hallway on a hard bench, awaiting his audience with the ambassador. He had a splitting headache and his mouth was dry, but more than anything, he was worried about Kiren. He could barely remember last night, and had awakened on some cot in the barn with blood matted in his hair. Had he been any place than at such a dignified party, he would have sworn someone hit him in the back of the head. But he knew he had drunk too much, which meant that he probably passed out and fell. Now he was just worried about his charge.

His concern did not lessen when he was ushered before the ambassador who sat regally in a chair and gazed at him with a glacial look of disapproval. He clutched his worn hat in his hands, his head bowed low.

"You must know," Maeva began, "how very important and valued is our relationship with the House of Storr. For decades, the Alfar have counted the Storr as their dearest allies and friends."

That was a bit of an exaggeration, Maeva thought to herself, but this oaf in front of her didn't know that.

"Yes, Ambassador," Oleif said humbly.

"Because of this, you can't imagine how distressed I was to find the young lady injured in the nearby woods."

"What?" Oleif exclaimed, terrified for his beloved charge.

"Yes," Maeva said sternly, "apparently someone plied her with drink, and she wandered away from the party. Her injuries are minor, thank the gods, and even now she's being tended by my personal physician."

"By all that is sacred," Oleif mumbled, holding his head in his hands. He had not wanted to come to this party but Kiren had been so excited, and against all his better judgment, he had relented. She was just blossoming into adulthood, but she had lived such a sheltered life. Her parents, especially her father, had begged him to keep her secluded, but his love for the young woman was such he would do anything for her.

"You can't imagine how disappointed I was for my guards to find you passed out in the barn. Really, this entire situation is unacceptable."

Oleif hung his head even lower.

"Until the young woman has completely recovered, she will remain in my care."

"That's not necessary," Oleif started to interject, but was cut short by Maeva.

"You're lucky I don't have you beaten and imprisoned. I doubt the imperials would look kindly on your incompetence, either."

That was finally enough for Oleif. "Very well, Ambassador. May I at least see Kiren before I go?"

"She's sleeping right now," Maeva said, "and I wish you to leave as soon as possible. She'll send word as soon as she's well."

Oleif did not like this at all, but the two, towering elven guards that flanked him silenced any protest he might have made. They escorted him out under the baleful gaze of the Alfar Ambassador, a look that transitioned to a pleased smile as soon as he was out of view.

Chapter 14

The breeze moved her dark hair across her forehead, which made Kiren stir then awaken. She looked about in confusion and with a little fear. She was not in her bedroom at home. She looked down at the soft bed clothes she was wearing, and although they fit her perfectly, they were not her clothes. There was a door to her right that was open, but there were two large elven guards standing outside of it. One glanced in, saw that she was awake, and made a signal to someone she could not see.

The beautiful elven woman came in, and a disarray of images rushed through Kiren's mind. The journey from her home, the party, the hallway, then the brutal and passionate encounter in the bed which was more disjointed than all the rest. She recalled the minor pain and the enormous pleasure that drowned out everything else, all sight and sound lost to that sensation.

Maeva looked down into those sapphire blue eyes and felt two emotions so unfamiliar to her she could barely identify them. One she recognized as regret and the second might have been guilt. Both, however, were for the way she had taken the young woman, not because of the actual taking.

"My servants will dress you," Maeva said, "then provide you with some activity as I'm very busy today."

Kiren didn't understand any of this. "Where is Oleif?"

"Your guardian got drunk and was very disruptive at the party. He has been dismissed."

The blue eyes clouded, then slid to the guards at the door, assessing the situation. "I should go."

"You may not," Maeva said calmly.

The blue eyes again flicked to the guards at the door. "I'm a prisoner?"

"You're my guest," Maeva replied, "but I will not allow you to leave."

Kiren looked down at her hands. That seemed to be a bit of splitting hairs and did not explain anything about her current predicament. She sighed, a gentle acquiescence that in anyone else would have looked feeble and pathetic and would have produced nothing but disdain from Maeva. But somehow the pensive compliance coupled with the faraway look in those blue eyes made Maeva want to take the young woman right back to bed, albeit more gently this time. She cursed the meetings she had scheduled this day, meetings she was tempted to postpone despite their importance.

"I'll see you at noon meal," Maeva said, then left before she gave in to her desire.

Two servants came in and the senior of the pair eyed the young lady. The dress she had worn the night before had been lovely enough, but the Alfar were famous for their splendid woven fabric and luxurious textiles. She knew exactly what she wanted to dress this one in, and because the girl resisted not at all, the deed was quickly done.

Melwen entered Maeva's chambers, a touch disgruntled that he was to play babysitter for the next few hours when there were so many more important things to do. He stopped abruptly, taking in the sight of Maeva's new lover. His mouth did not move as he was master of Alfar impassivity, but there was a look of approval in his eyes. He bowed to her respectfully and motioned for her to precede him through the door, which she did as the two guards fell in behind them.

Maeva glanced up as the procession started down the stairs, and she, too, stopped abruptly. Kiren was now dressed in pants, a blouse, and a jacket, all an iridescent blue that perfectly matched her eyes. The outfit was casual wear, but the young woman wore it with such refinement and grace she looked like royalty. And Maeva, who was biased toward the Alfar in all things, thought that none of her people could wear the outfit better.

She became aware that the guards at her side were also staring with uncharacteristic unprofessionalism, and when they became aware that she was aware, they snapped back to attention, eyes forward. Melwen paused their procession and approached Maeva. She did not take her eyes from her little prize as she spoke to him.

"Why don't you take her into the main hall and see if you can't find her some sort of bauble as a gift?"

"Of course," Melwen said, and Maeva left for her meeting, barely able to take her eyes from Kiren.

Melwen escorted Kiren into the main hall, a museum of sorts with various artifacts and jewelry on display. He had thought it an easy enough task to find the young woman a gift, for humans were known for their avarice and love of shiny things. So, it was with growing consternation that he watched her wander about the room, admiring the architecture but showing little beyond polite interest in the various items he presented for her inspection. Maeva would not be pleased if the girl did not accept anything, and he wasn't even sure Kiren understood he was trying to provide her with a present. He continued to escalate his offerings, moving to ever more extravagant pieces. But even when he took a diamond necklace from a locked chest and held it before her, she examined it politely, if a bit clueless, then glanced away with a disinterest she was not devious enough to fake and guileless enough not to hide.

Melwen was beginning to despair, for Maeva's anger could be swift and disproportionate to even minor failure, when the young woman's eyes lit up and she moved swiftly across the room. There was a worn book on a shelf which she removed eagerly. She opened it, but then her expression fell. Melwen felt the oddest tug in his chest at the crestfallen look.

"What's wrong?" he asked.

"I've read this one," Kiren said with disappointment.

"You like books?" Melwen said hopefully.

"Oh yes."

"Then come with me."

Kiren followed him down another hallway, into a large room, and she stopped, her eyes wide and shining with wonderment. There were shelves on the walls from floor to ceiling and the shelves were full of books, more than she had thought existed. She moved to the nearest shelf, caressing the spines of the tomes, her expression one almost of worship. Melwen observed her reaction with amazement and relief: amazed because he had assumed as a human, she was illiterate, and relief because, although it wasn't exactly according to Maeva's direction, it was something she wanted.

She began picking and choosing amongst the volumes, and when she struggled to juggle them in her arms, one of the guards moved forward to help her.

"Why don't you just take what you can read today?" Melwen suggested. "And we can come back tomorrow."

"Really?" Kiren said brightly, and then pulled four more heavy tomes from the shelves. Melwen observed the response and almost smiled.

He escorted the young lady back to Maeva's chambers and without hesitation she climbed into one of the oversized chairs that made her look even smaller than she was. But the extra space allowed her to surround herself with her beloved books and they were piled about her as she began voraciously reading. And Melwen stared in wonder at the little beauty who had been kidnapped, violated, and now imprisoned, and who seemed oblivious to all of that as she lost herself in the world of literature.

The meetings had gone much longer than Maeva anticipated and she missed the noon meal. Although her thoughts were very much on the petite woman in her room, she did not get the chance to see her until evening. Melwen greeted her upon her return.

"Did she find something she liked?" Maeva asked.

"See for yourself," Melwen said.

Kiren sat in the chair, her legs tucked beneath her, surrounded by piles of books. She was so engrossed in the activity she did not look up, even at their quiet conversation.

"She wanted books?" Maeva said in disbelief.

"Yes," Melwen said. "Books."

Maeva approached the young woman, who looked up with that air of gentleness. Maeva started to speak but one book at Kiren's elbow caught her eye. She picked it up.

"You're reading this?" Maeva asked.

"No," Kiren said, and Maeva started to put the book back down, relieved. Her relief was short-lived. "I already finished that one."

Maeva could not disguise her skepticism. "You can read the ancient Alfar language, High Elvish?"

"Yes," Kiren said, as if it were no matter, as if she were not claiming an ability that ninety-nine percent of the Alfar themselves did not possess. Ancient Alfar was a convoluted, complex, highly symbolic language that few could master.

"And can you speak it?" Maeva said, switching to the ancient tongue since she was one of the few who had mastered it.

"Of course," Kiren said, effortlessly switching to the tongue herself.

"And who taught you this language?" Maeva said, still in the ancient language.

"My father did," Kiren explained in flawless Elvish. "He was a great admirer of Thar'rath, who advocated learning multiple languages."

Maeva was well-familiar with Thar'rath, for he was an esteemed elven scholar who considered linguistic ability a crucial skill. But she was still skeptical and would test the depth of the girl's knowledge.

"And why did Thar'rath advocate such a skill?"

The blue eyes looked up at her, gentle but enigmatic. "So he could better know the mind of his enemy."

Maeva realized she was holding her breath, for although the statement held no threat or recrimination, it was devastatingly, sweepingly matter of fact. It was a display of subtle, utter power from one thought powerless. But Kiren simply returned to the book in her hand, brushing her fingers over the page, as if the power did not even matter.

Maeva looked to the other books surrounding Kiren, realizing they encompassed multiple tongues.

"How many languages do you speak?" Maeva asked.

Kiren had to think about it. "Six," she said, "No, seven. And several dialects of Dverger, which really are almost like a separate language." She then rattled off a list that would have shamed the most prestigious linguists among the Alfar. "I think that's it," she said, wrinkling her brow.

Maeva just looked at her. "Were you planning on having a lot of enemies?" she said at last.

This elicited a giggle from Kiren, a beautiful, musical little burst of laughter. And Maeva found the response utterly charming, so unaffected and pure, a response Kiren did not restrain despite her current circumstances because it was her nature to laugh when she found something funny.

"Why don't you put your books away," Maeva said, and Kiren looked up at the sudden intensity in her tone, an intensity matched by that in her eyes. Maeva had planned to have dinner with her, but now her plans had changed. She took Kiren by the hand and glanced to Melwen, who nodded his goodnight and took his leave, leaving the doors open behind him. He glanced to the guards who nodded to him. He understood this was rapidly becoming a desired post, although to his mind it would be torturous listening without being able to watch.

Maeva led the young woman to her bed and very slowly undressed her, then removed her own clothing. Kiren looked upon her shyly, curiously, and Maeva encouraged her bashful exploration. And the younger woman responded, not unwillingly as she had done the night before, but more freely, at first with hesitation, then with growing passion. And although Maeva knew that Kiren was inexperienced, she was not unskilled, possessing a remarkable instinct as to what would bring Maeva pleasure. And in the end, the Alfar High Ambassador, future Directorate of the Elven High Council, spent hours making love to her petite little treasure, and Maeva, who had loved nothing in her life and discarded everything, determined she would never let this one go.

The Alfar Embassy received its first missive from the empire within days. It politely inquired as to the status and well-being of the heir to the House of Storr. The Alfar Embassy replied just as politely that the heir to the House of Storr, although young, was legally an adult, was currently enjoying the hospitality of the Alfar Ambassador, was in good health, and that the empire needn't concern itself with such matters. The next imperial missive was slightly more strongly worded, reminding the Alfar Ambassador that the House of Storr lie within imperial territory and that its heir was an imperial citizen. The embassy replied that the Alfar had long enjoyed a friendship and alliance with the House of Storr, and that such an arrangement was likely to continue even with the deaths of the Lord and Lady Storr. The wording of the next imperial missive escalated the situation further by demanding an audience with the heir to the House of Storr to ensure her presence within the Alfar embassy was voluntary, at which time the embassy responded by claiming grievous injury at such an insulting implication, and broke off communication.

It was within this context that Kiren disappeared.

Maeva had allowed the young woman a little more freedom about the estate although she was still heavily guarded everywhere she went. Melwen explained to Kiren that this was for her safety, but he was hard-pressed to explain what she was in danger from. The constant vigilance seemed overdone because the diminutive woman was wholly placid, and the thought of her attempting to escape was ludicrous. Which is why Melwen's first thought when Kiren disappeared was that somehow the imperials had infiltrated the compound and made off with her.

"Have you searched everywhere?" Maeva demanded, coming down the steps into the estate courtyard.

"Yes," Melwen replied, far more calmly than he felt, "I've ordered a second pass of the entire embassy grounds."

Maeva was furious. It had to have been the imperials. There was no way that docile little creature had run away. She would not admit that the thought of Kiren fleeing was the worse of the two possibilities because it felt like betrayal.

"Who was on guard duty?"

Melwen had the man brought forward and Maeva slapped him across the face. "Where did you see her last?"

Even though he was terrified of Maeva, the guard's impassive expression did not waver. "She was right here in the middle of the courtyard with a full contingent. She was picking flowers over there, and when I turned back to look at her, she was gone."

Maeva whirled back upon Melwen. "Has anyone come in or out today? Has there been a full roll call of all staff?"

"No one has come in or out," Melwen responded, "and the roll call is nearly complete with none missing."

"How is this possible?" Maeva said, her fury growing unabated.

Before Melwen could respond, an excited voice came from the stable.

"Over here!"

All rushed toward the voice, led by Maeva who pushed past the throng hovering in the doorway. She felt a cold, unreasonable fear, certain the young woman had been trampled by a horse. She stopped abruptly.

Kiren was sound asleep in the hay, buried under a blanket of puppies draped about her small form. The tiny hounds were but two days old and the mother softly growled at the interlopers from the corner. But she did not count Kiren amongst the intruders, and the little beasts were perfectly content to sprawl about her sleepily.

Maeva controlled herself with great effort. She wanted to run to the girl, to pick her up and confirm that she was all right. But that would have gone against all Alfar decorum, so she took a deep breath and maintained her icy reserve.

"Bring her," she ordered, and spun about on her heel.

Melwen gently awakened Kiren, who looked to him with no understanding of what was happening. He helped her to her feet and brushed her off, then escorted her out of the stable. She was confused, because the entire courtyard was filled with embassy personnel, especially guards, and one of them was being tied to a stake.

"What's happening?" she asked.

"We couldn't find you, which is a serious breach in security. That man was responsible for watching you and now must be punished."

"No!" Kiren cried out and stepped forward. But Melwen restrained her. Maeva stood across from them and did not look over at the anguished cry.

"I promise I won't leave!"

Maeva's eyes slid to her and Melwen held up his hand, a subtle gesture that halted the beating.

"What?" Maeva said quietly, easily heard because the courtyard had grown silent.

"I promise I won't leave," Kiren said, "please just don't hurt him."

Maeva gazed at her. "I have your word?"

"You have my word."

"Very well," Maeva said, and gestured for the man to be released. She stepped in front of Kiren and her tone was firm. "I want you to go up to your room."

Kiren took one last look at the guard who had been about to be punished, then turned and started up the steps, accompanied by a guard detail even larger than normal. Maeva waited until she was out of earshot, then turned back to Melwen.

"You will proceed with the beating as ordered. Just make certain you're out of sight and hearing of the house."

Melwen nodded and Maeva started up the steps after Kiren.

Her anger was still fierce when Maeva walked into her room, but it was tempered when she looked at Kiren who stood by the bookshelf, running her fingers over the leather tomes. The young woman was distressed by what had happened, that was evident. Maeva sighed and sat down in one of the chairs.

"Come here."

Kiren obeyed, tentative and distraught, and she did not resist when Maeva pulled her onto her lap.

"You're trembling," Maeva said, genuinely dismayed.

"I didn't want you to hurt that man because of me."

Maeva at last understood how very gentle this young woman was. She brushed the raven hair from those troubled blue eyes, and again felt those unfamiliar emotions of guilt and regret. If she could turn back the hands of time, she would do so in order to start anew with this one.

"I'm sorry I caused you pain the first time."

Kiren did not at first comprehend what she was talking about, but then understood. "Is it not always painful for a woman her first time?"

Maeva wanted to smile, for this girl hardly seemed a woman, although in truth she was.

"Yes," Maeva said, "but I should have been more gentle with you. I promise I'll not hurt you again. I want only to bring you pleasure."

The blue eyes were so dark they were almost black. They assessed Maeva, her words, her demeanor, then very slowly, she leaned forward and touched her lips to Maeva's. The soft, feathery feeling violently aroused Maeva but she restrained herself, using every bit of her Alfar control. She returned the gentle kiss, feeling the hesitant probing of the tip of the tongue as it parted her lips. The kiss deepened, then grew prolonged, and her hand drifted down between Kiren's legs, caressing her. She slipped her fingers inside the pants, then inside the girl as those little hips responded and a soft, muffled moan came from Kiren. Maeva's kiss grew only slightly harder as she used every ounce of restraint, one hand cradling Kiren's shoulders, one hand pleasuring her between her legs, and her tongue ever-so-gently dominating her mouth. And the body responded, rising up to meet her hand in a matching rhythm. And Maeva brought the young woman to climax with no thought of her own, wanting only to banish her sadness and fear forever.

Chapter 15

Maeva and Melwen sat in the library quietly going over the final details of the Dverger treaty. They would first meet up with the Deep Miners, a group of dwarves who had not yet agreed to an alliance with the Alfar. It was widely understood they would go along with their dwarven brethren, but they were a proud people, an offshoot, and therefore it was important to meet with them face-to-face as a sign of respect. Lorifal had assured her that it was simply a matter of going through the motions, and that once the Deep Miners had agreed, the larger Dverger treaty would be signed.

Maeva's eyes, as they so often did, drifted over to Kiren. They had fallen into a pattern of sorts, with the young woman content to pass the time with her books or her artwork or her music. Not only was she a gifted scholar, she was a talented artist and a brilliant musician. It was hard for Maeva to fathom that the girl had never left her home. In response to Maeva's mild probing, Kiren divulged that she had lived a totally secluded life with only her mother and father and a small staff on their estate. When her parents had passed due to illness, Oleif had stayed on as steward to manage her affairs as best he could. Apparently, her mother was the one with business sense and had made extensive arrangements so that the fortunes of the House of Storr continued to grow and perpetuate themselves, so Oleif had only to care for Kiren. And Kiren seemed to have little grasp of how wealthy she was, or how incredibly valuable the land she owned was.

Or perhaps she didn't care, Maeva thought, examining the raven-haired beauty. Although Kiren loved to talk of literature, art, and music, it was difficult to draw her into a political discussion. That wouldn't have been that unusual, given her personality, but the few times Maeva had managed to elicit an opinion from her, Kiren was startling astute, revealing a breath-taking breadth of knowledge as deep as it was wide. Perhaps it was because she was such an avid student of history, but she had a geopolitical understanding of Arianthem that was astonishing. Maeva was glad the imperials had not discovered this formidable little creature.

While Maeva watched Kiren, Melwen watched her. Outwardly, little had changed with Maeva. Those who observed the two together saw Maeva as very strict with the young woman and exceedingly possessive. He was firmly convinced that Maeva would take the Alfar to war against the empire before she would give the girl up. Which made their next task very difficult.

"The Deep Miners wish to meet in Matting's Depth."

"That's expected," Maeva replied. "It's a historically significant site to them."

Melwen's attention moved to the one across the room. "Our intelligence reports indicate the empire has moved a sizeable force between us and the Depth."

"Yes," Maeva said, examining her long fingernails. "The traitor in our midst has been busy."

There was a spy in the embassy, but one of which they were well aware. Maeva used the turncoat to her advantage, forwarding whatever information or misinformation she wished to the imperials. She would enjoy killing the woman when she was through with her, but right now she was too valuable a resource.

"Make preparations to leave with an enormous force."

"And what are you going to do with her?" Melwen asked, nodding to Kiren.

"I'm taking her with me, of course," Maeva said.

That seemed risky to Melwen, but no less risky than leaving Kiren at the embassy. There really weren't any good options about what to do with her, and a confrontation with the empire, whether now or later, was becoming inevitable.

Feyden entered Fireside with much on his mind. Raine was waiting for him, having sensed her friend's disquiet in their earlier, cryptic exchange. He had been willing to say little in the open, and was a little taken aback that someone else would be present for their conversation. A woman with startling blue-green eyes was in the main hall, and she rose gracefully from the settee to greet him.

"Feyden, I know this is unexpected, but the Lady Jorden is a friend of your sister and may help provide some insight into what's going on."

"That would be unusual for many reasons," Feyden said skeptically, "foremost in that my sister counts few among humankind as her friends."

Jorden was not offended by his skepticism. "Well, there are few humans who are also secretly the head of the Guild of Thieves."

"Ah," Feyden said, his demeanor changing instantly, "you're Lagmann. Yes, Maeva speaks highly of you."

Raine did not wish to waste time on niceties. She was tiring of the continued intricacies of diplomacy. Were it not for Weynild's constant encouragement, she would leave all these parties to themselves and go fight the Hyr'rok'kin alone. But Weynild, in her wise and steely manner always brought Raine back on course.

"So, Feyden, tell me why the imperials and the Alfar are suddenly at one another's throats at a time when I'm trying to arrange an alliance."

Feyden sat down heavily in front of the fire. "I'm not entirely certain. I haven't spoken with Maeva personally and her letters are obscure, which means she believes they may be intercepted. But she's done something so strange and unexpected, I don't know how to interpret it."

"You're talking about the heir to the House of Storr," Raine said.

"Yes," Feyden replied, "the official story is that she's taken the young woman into her care due to injury, but Maeva is not known as an angel of mercy and the story is at odds with the fact that she now won't release her, or even allow the imperials to see her."

"Then she's kidnapped her," Raine said. "The House of Storr are the largest landholders in Arianthem and their lands border all of the high country."

"That makes no sense," Feyden said. "There are so many better ways the compliance of the House of Storr could have been continued. And what's to stop the empire from taking over those lands if they think the woman is being held captive? I think this Emperor would welcome an opportunity to add to his holdings."

"Which would completely provoke the Alfar," Raine said.

"Which may have been Maeva's intent all along."

Frustration was evident on Raine's face. "Then she's made her decision, and it's not in the empire's favor. I still don't understand why she's baiting them to war, though."

"Might I interject?" Jorden said. "There may be another explanation for this." She turned to Feyden pointedly. "You're aware of your sister's, how shall we say this, tendencies?"

"What do you mean?" Feyden asked.

"Well, let's put it this way. Kiren, the heir to the House of Storr, is a tiny little thing. A woman, but barely, and looks younger than she actually is. She is stunningly beautiful with jet black hair and eyes so blue they're almost the color of Raine's." She paused, because Raine's eyes were very gray right now. "At least when Raine is not angry like she is at the moment."

This seemed totally irrelevant to Raine, but Feyden had a look of growing comprehension on his face. "Surely she did not..." he muttered.

"I think she did."

"What?" Raine asked. "What did she do or not do?"

"I'm fairly certain she took that young woman to her bed."

"What?" Raine said in disbelief, and Feyden was no less incredulous.

"You're describing exactly Maeva's type, but among the Alfar, not humans. Maeva detests humans and I can't imagine her being attracted to one. And even if she did bed the girl, Maeva tires of her lovers and quickly discards them, so I can't think she's holding this woman for some romantic purpose."

"I have to agree with Feyden," Raine said, "I've seen Maeva and she's unrelenting when she sees something she wants, consequences be damned. But this doesn't sound like something she would do."

"And you didn't see the way Maeva looked at the young woman the night of the party," Jorden replied. "I've seen looks of lust and looks of desire, but—," she trailed off, looking at Raine.

"What?" Raine asked.

"The only time I've seen a look like that is when your dragon lover looks at you."

The Alfar procession was magnificent, as splendid and intimidating as the one that had initially left the mountains. The imperial force approaching them was equal in size, but still, they were daunted by the diplomatic convoy that appeared more a conquering army than an ambassador on a mission of peace. The convoy slowed to a halt and two knight commanders at the head of the imperial force approached on horseback. The female initiated contact with the forward troops.

"I wish to speak to the Alfar Ambassador," Nerthus said coldly. She was surprised when her Alfar counterpart merely nodded and gestured. A path opened up through the middle of the elven soldiers, and Nerthus, Bristol, and a few high-ranking imperial soldiers rode through the throng to the well-guarded carriage. The door to the carriage opened, and an elven male who was definitely not the Alfar Ambassador stepped down.

"May I help you?" Melwen asked politely.

"Where is the Ambassador?" Nerthus demanded.

"She's on her way to finalize the treaty with the Dverger. She has kept the empire well-informed of her whereabouts and her schedule."

The procession was a decoy, Nerthus thought angrily. Somehow Maeva had known of their intent to intercept her and had sent out the convoy as a distraction. It was likely the sly elf had already left imperial territory by some back route with a skeleton force. She was partially right as Maeva had not yet left imperial lands but was miles away where she had stopped their small force in an idyllic setting by a gurgling brook. She was currently having a picnic lunch in the pastoral setting and intended to take her young lover on a blanket in the grass before they continued on.

"This is outrageous," Bristol said, "where is the heir to the House of Storr?"

"I assure you the woman is safe and her presence with the Ambassador is voluntary," Melwen replied. That last part was almost true. The girl was so meek that "voluntary" did not have a great deal of meaning.

The response drew Bristol's ire, but before the situation could escalate further, Melwen proffered the olive branch Maeva had directed him to give.

"Once the Dverger treaty is signed, the Ambassador will travel to the land of the Ha'kan. She suggests the Emperor send a contingency to meet her there where she will provide complete and unrestricted access to Kiren.

The Emperor's representatives can verify that the young woman is safe and not a captive."

This was unacceptable to Bristol, and he started to bluster a response when quite amazingly, Nerthus held up her hand.

"Wait," she said, thinking furiously. Just last night, after pulling Idonea into an alcove and engaging in a frenzied, dangerous, exhilarating romp, Idonea had fondly run her fingers through Nerthus' blonde hair and then informed her with a degree of regret that she would be leaving soon for the Ha'kan capital. Her duties with Kelsey were finished and she had to move on to her next task.

"That will be acceptable," Nerthus found herself saying.

"What?" Bristol sputtered.

Nerthus turned to him. "There's no sense in escalating this situation further if it can be resolved diplomatically," she said. "I'll go to the Ha'kan capital myself to see first-hand that this imperial citizen acts of her own volition. A few weeks' time is but a small inconvenience if this proves to be a misunderstanding."

Bristol stared at her in disbelief and Melwen's astonishment was just as great. Their intelligence reports indicated this woman was the least likely of the Emperor's command staff to provide any sort of measured response.

"Excellent," he said, bowing low. "The Alfar will welcome the esteemed Knight Commander's presence."

Nerthus wheeled her horse about, her cheeks a trifle red. She wasn't sure how she was going to sell this to the Emperor, but fortunately he heeded her advice on almost everything. She put her heels into her horse's flank because she did not want to face Bristol's questioning right now.

She needn't have worried. Bristol was so flabbergasted by her behavior he did not know what to say, anyway. He was quite certain something had addled her brain, although he had to admit, the change wasn't entirely unpleasant.

Chapter 16

The great hall of Matting's Depth was elaborately decorated for the prestigious ceremony. The Deep Miners did not wish their Alfar brethren to think them inhospitable or uncouth, and they had gone to great lengths to provide a proper setting for the formal ceremony.

And Maeva had to admit they had done a good job. The dwarves understood the importance of heritage and culture, unlike the sons of men who had memories as short as their lives. But, as she glanced down at the diminutive dark-haired beauty at her side, so fetchingly dressed in the raiment of the Alfar, she also had to admit she was softening towards the humans. Any race that could produce that magical little creature could not be all bad.

Kiren took a seat on a bench against the wall. Few were allowed to be present at the final negotiations, but Maeva sensed Kiren's considerable interest in the proceedings and made arrangements for her to watch. As always, she was flanked by her elven guards.

The Dverger contingent entered in a dignified procession. They were dressed in heavy armor, but it was the elaborately decorated heavy armor meant for social engagements, not warfare. It was designed to showcase the two great accomplishments of the Deep Miners: their acquisition of rare ores from the depths of the earth, and their skill in smithing that ore into just about anything. Maeva greeted them with great gravitas, and they returned the greeting solemnly. All sat down at the round table, the dwarven chief flanked by his closest advisors on one side, and Maeva, her advisors, and an interpreter on the other. Maeva spoke the common dialect of Dverger, but there were some intricacies to the Deep Miner tongue that required careful translation, so Maeva had decided to conduct the entire negotiation through an interpreter.

"We greet our dwarven brothers and sisters," Maeva began, "and we commend the generous spirit with which they have approached this alliance."

The Deep Miners were the most xenophobic of all dwarves and none spoke the elven tongue. So, they turned to look expectantly at the interpreter who dutifully and sonorously translated Maeva's words. A strange look passed over the dwarven's chiefs features.

Kiren made a small, muffled noise and the elven guard at her side looked down. The young woman had promised to be quiet, and in a most unusual display of disobedience, was already flirting with breaking that promise.

"It is this magnanimous spirit," Maeva continued, "that is so greatly admired and welcomed by the Alfar." She turned to the interpreter who again pompously translated her words.

The dwarven chief frowned and several of his advisors shifted in their chairs as Maeva felt a trace of unease. A snort of muffled laughter came from the bench against the wall and Maeva looked over at Kiren with disapproval. Her elven guards shifted, ready to remove her if need-be. The dwarven chief's eyes flicked to the girl sitting on the bench, then he glowered at Maeva.

Maeva had no choice but to continue with her prepared opening, uncertain why this seemed to be unraveling. "This spirit, although ever-present in the Dverger people, has never been more fully on display than it is now at this point in history."

The translator spoke in a flowery manner, attempting to win back his audience, but instead he pushed them over the edge. Kiren simply burst into laughter as the dwarven chief slammed his fist down onto the table and leaped to his feet. A sharp clang of steel rang out as his advisors sprang up and drew their weapons and another clang as the elven guards followed suit, drawing their swords. Everyone stood tensely facing one another. Kiren also jumped up, somehow eluding her guards and coming to the table, her hands raised in a soothing motion to the dwarves. She spoke rapid-fire to the dwarven chief in Dverger, far more fluently than the interpreter, and he paused as weapons wavered in the air throughout the hall. She pointed to the translator, then looked back at the chief, explained something else to him in the dwarven tongue, then shook her head. The chief appeared skeptical, but her words had a calming effect on him, and his advisors lowered their weapons. Kiren glanced at the interpreter, then made some off-hand comment, shrugging her shoulders, and the dwarven chief burst into laughter, pounding on the table with his fists in delight. His advisors also roared with laughter.

"Kiren," Maeva demanded, "what's happening?"

Kiren told the dwarven chief she was going to explain to the Alfar Ambassador what had occurred, and he nodded his understanding and took his seat. She then switched tongues, now speaking in Elvish as opposed to the common language.

"The interpreter wasn't translating your words correctly. Instead of 'spirit' he was using the term for 'nose,' and so the Dverger thought you were going on at great lengths about the size of their noses."

Maeva paled. This was a grave insult to the dwarves and insulting a dwarf's nose was one of the worst slurs in their culture. She might as well have declared war on them; it would have been taken less seriously.

"And what did you tell them?"

"I explained the mistake and told them what you meant to say."

Maeva's eyes were on the dwarven chief, who was watching Kiren. Although he could not speak Elvish, Kiren tended to speak with her hands as well as her mouth when switching between languages, and he followed the conversation, nodding in agreement.

"And what did you say at the end that made them laugh?"

Kiren blushed a little. "I told him at least the interpreter didn't express admiration for the size of their mines, um, as the Dverger word 'shaft' is very close to the slang word for a man's privates." She blushed again, "It's very typically dwarven humor."

Maeva stared down at the little beauty. Kiren had just saved years of negotiation by catching the error, then topped it off by winning back the Dverger with a clever pun that showed her understanding of both their language and culture. The chief said something, pointing at Kiren, then something else, pointing at the interpreter. He scowled at the man who had looked horrified since Kiren had interrupted.

"He says that he likes me," Kiren said, "but he doesn't like him. And he wants him to leave."

Maeva made a dismissive gesture and the man fairly fled the hall. Kiren watched, concerned, hoping the interpreter wouldn't get in trouble. Maeva sat back down and gestured to the now-empty interpreter seat.

"If you wouldn't mind," she said drily, and Kiren happily took the seat. This was all very exciting.

And so the negotiations began again, this time facilitated by Kiren who moved so effortlessly between the Elvish and Dverger tongues it was almost as if Maeva and the dwarven chief were speaking directly. And Kiren was able to translate not only Maeva's words but her intentions, utilizing the full richness of both languages. And it was clear the dwarven chief had taken a liking to Kiren, as had the entire dwarven contingent, and almost all of the issues were quickly resolved.

There was one last, thorny issue, however, that was a sticking point. Kiren thought this was a shame as it was apparent that both the Dverger and Alfar wanted the same thing. They had resolved all their mutual aid issues, divided up their shared resources, and determined to provide a united front against the Hyr'rok'kin. But there was one last piece of disputed land that was problematic, which was unfortunate in Kiren's view because everything else had gone so well. And although her father had taught her that an interpreter should never involve themselves personally in the conversation, this was an issue that seemed to have an obvious solution, at least to her. The conversation died, and both parties looked across the table with frustration, so Kiren decided to say something. She leaned toward Maeva and spoke quietly in the Alfar high tongue so that only she and Maeva would understand.

"Why don't you offer them the Red Deep?"

Maeva's impulse was to chastise Kiren for saying anything at the table that was not a direct translation, but she stopped. It was a brilliant suggestion. The Red Deep was not particularly valuable to the Alfar, but it held great symbolic meaning to the Deep Miners as it was the site of the birth of one of their first chieftains. It was something the Deep Miners were too proud to ask for and something the Alfar would not think to offer, but the symbolism of the proposal might sway the dwarves. It was a suggestion that only an impartial, extraordinarily knowledgeable student of history would make.

With the way Maeva was staring at her, Kiren thought for certain she was in trouble, but she would not back down from the suggestion. Maeva, on the other hand, had never seen any stubbornness in Kiren and was admiring the way it gave her lower lip a pouty look. None of this was apparent in her icy, Alfar exterior. It simply looked like she was spending an extended period of time making up her mind.

"Very well," Maeva said at last, "make them the offer."

The dwarves grew very contemplative as Kiren laid out the proposal, looking to one another and nodding. The chieftain was very impressed with the deference the offer implied. He spoke in Dverger while Kiren listened carefully, then she translated his words.

"He says this offer is truly welcome to the Deep Miners for it displays the Ambassador's great understanding and appreciation of their history. The Ambassador is as wise as she is generous."

Maeva could not help but note Kiren's dry tone at this last sentence. She spoke at a normal volume while looking across the table at the dwarves.

"In half an hour you're going to be face-down in my bed spread-eagle, bound, and naked."

Maeva's tone was so conversational in nature Kiren actually began translating Maeva's words before their meaning sunk in and she realized the words were for her. The guards behind them strained to control their reactions because Maeva was speaking the common Elvish they could understand. Melwen also sought to maintain his impassive expression.

"Do you want me to translate that?" Kiren said with a trace of sarcasm.

"If you wish," Maeva said, pleased with herself. The dwarven chieftain was looking at Kiren expectantly, so she made up something about the long and prosperous relationship the Dverger and Alfar were going to enjoy. He responded, and Kiren started to translate, then clamped her jaw shut. He waved her on, encouraging her to translate his words.

"What did he say?" Maeva asked.

Kiren sighed. "He says the Alfar interpreter is as brilliant as she is beautiful."

"Half an hour," Maeva said, reiterating Kiren's fate.

The negotiations ended, the treaty was signed, and as promised, within half an hour Maeva had pinned her little lover face-down in bed, joyfully, teasingly "punishing" her for her impudence, bringing the young woman to several shuddering climaxes while the poor Alfar guards stared ahead at nothing, only able to imagine what was happening right behind them.

Chapter 17

Skye's horse picked its way through the forest, and Skye sat pleasantly slumped in the seat, letting her natural balance keep her upright in a relaxed position. Torsten rode next to her, and Aeric and Flint behind her. They had brought down enough game in the last few days to feed an entire village for weeks. They had chased some bandits from the eastern fringes, tracked and slain a particularly troublesome panther, and cleared out a small pocket of Hyr'rok'kin Shards. Skye had traveled the extent of her lands, reconnected with her people, and rejuvenated herself by spending time in the deep woods. It had been a wonderful time, and part of her longed to stay in her beloved forest. But part of her missed her friends and lovers and she was anxious to return to the Ha'kan capital. Once again, she thanked the gods that events had worked out so that she could have both worlds.

A finger of unease traced its way down her spine, and she turned on her horse to look behind her. Torsten caught the gesture, and in fact had now seen her do it several times over the past few days. He did not hear or see anything, but Skye's senses were better than his. Still, he was not greatly troubled because Skye was not concerned, just a little bemused.

"What is it, Skye?" he asked.

"It's the strangest thing," Skye said. "I don't hear anything. I don't see or smell anything. Yet I have the oddest sensation that something is following me."

Torsten turned on his horse to look behind them. "Another panther perhaps? The mate of the first?"

Skye shook her head. "No, it's nothing like that. It's—," her voice trailed off. "It's nothing. I'm sure I'm imagining things."

Raine was sound asleep when a presence in her room awakened her. Her impulse was to reach for her sword, but she stayed her hand.

"Raine," Idonea whispered. She doubted she could sneak up on Raine unawares, but she knew better than to startle her from sleep.

"What is it?" Raine said, "Is everything all right?"

"Yes," Idonea said, "I mean, no."

Raine sat up and lit a candle on her nightstand. "What's wrong?"

Idonea sat down on the edge of the bed. "All day long I had a feeling of unease, but I couldn't place the source."

"And?" Raine prompted.

"I just had a dream."

Idonea now had Raine's full attention. Neither Weynild nor her daughter had simple dreams. They had visions, premonitions, revelations, but never simple dreams.

"What was the dream about?"

"I'm not sure," Idonea said, frustrated, "but it was dark and frightening."

Raine's concern grew, for it took a great deal to frighten Idonea. Idonea raised her dark eyes to her, deadly serious.

"You need to get to the land of the Ha'kan as soon as possible."

The reunion with the Ha'kan was as passionate as always, and after a few days, Skye transitioned back to her more "civilized" ways. Still, the heightened sense of awareness that took hold of her in her forest stayed with her, as did the vague feeling of unease. Both Dallan and Rika had commented on it, but it was Senta whom it bothered the most. She had waited for Skye to spend her first few nights with her cohort, then invited the young woman to her chambers, an invitation Skye eagerly accepted.

And Skye finally generated the courage to ask to use her harness with Senta, who gladly consented, and the two spent hours having thunderous, playful sex. At the end, both fell asleep, exhausted, but Senta had awakened several times at Skye's tossing and turning. This was very unusual for the young woman, who generally slept so soundly she was immobile. Senta finally had to wrap herself around Skye to make her relax and fall into a deeper sleep.

Even now, Senta watched Skye from the balcony of the palace. The fair-haired one was walking across the tiled square in front of the immense staircase leading up to the royal hall. She appeared distracted and had a bit of a frown on her face, something very unusual for her. She stopped, looked behind her, and seemed a trifle irritated when there was nothing there.

"Is something wrong?" Queen Halla said, coming to Senta's side on the balcony. Her eyes sought out the object of Senta's attention.

"Something is bothering Skye," Senta said. "She's uneasy. Both Dallan and Rika have commented on it, and Skye herself has said she keeps feeling as if something is following her."

"Lifa has commented on it as well," Halla said. "She reported that Skye is sleeping poorly, something that's very rare for her."

Halla's eyes drifted across the square. Her daughter, accompanied by Rika, was trying to catch up with Skye.

"And look at Gimle," Senta said, and Halla's eyes drifted to the other side of the square. Gimle was standing under a tree, a pensive look on her face as she, too, watched Skye. The scholar examined the empty area behind Skye, the area that Skye herself seemed bothered by, and Gimle cocked her head to one side.

Halla had a terrible premonition, and her First General, who gave little credence to such forebodings, felt the same.

"Something's wrong," Senta said. She moved to the circular staircase that spiraled down from the balcony and began taking the stairs in great leaps. Gimle had also started moving towards Skye, who now stood stopped in the center of the empty square as if frozen in place. Astrid came out onto the balcony to Queen Halla's side, and Dallan and Rika, who did not share Senta's or Gimle's concern, at least shared their confusion. Skye looked lost standing in the middle of the square. Dallan saw Senta reach the bottom of the stairs and begin moving toward Skye, not running, but striding at a brisk pace. Gimle, too, was now moving toward Skye.

"Something's wrong," Dallan said. "Look at Senta and Gimle." Rika did not hesitate but grabbed Dallan's arm.

"Let's go!"

Skye saw none of this. Rather she was stopped, deeply concentrating. Something was here. She could not see it, she could not hear it, but she could feel it. A smell, something like the sulfur that Gimle had in her alchemy lab, made her nose twitch. And then Gimle, bizarrely, as if her thoughts had conjured her out of thin air, was right in front of her, grabbing her arm and pulling her to her. And Senta was there as well, followed by Dallan and Rika. Everyone was agitated except Skye, who felt numb and could not figure out how everyone had just materialized from nothingness. Her head hurt.

"Gimle what is it?" Senta asked urgently.

"I don't know," Gimle said calmly, but Senta had heard this calmness in Gimle's voice before: it was the composed demeanor she displayed before battle. Senta drew her greatsword, looking about them, and Dallan and Rika followed suit, drawing their swords at whatever unseen threat had roused Senta. They were confused but they would follow the First General without question.

"What's happening?" Halla murmured fearfully from the balcony.

"Look there," Astrid said. A group of Ha'kan soldiers had seen their fearsome First General draw a weapon and ran to join the fight against whatever threatened her. But something was keeping them from entering the tiled square, some barrier that could not be seen or penetrated.

"It's like an invisible wall, something magical." Astrid said. She was growing more convinced of the presence of great peril. "There's something terrible here, something evil."

"Could it be that sorceress, Ingrid?" Halla said.

"I don't know," Astrid replied.

Gimle felt a deep sense of foreboding and coolly crushed the dread that fought to rise in her. It was almost here.

"By the gods," Dallan exclaimed, "what is that?"

A bluish, smoky cloud rose up out of the ground, formed a pillar, then began to solidify into a hideous black mass. A great tooth-filled maw opened, and the Reaper Shard screamed, a horrifying sound that made Skye tremble and cover her ears. She was terrified right now, and there were only two times in her life she could remember being this afraid: the first when she was chased by a bear as a child, and the second when she, Dallan, and Rika had been ambushed by Hyr'rok'kin while still at the Academy. Gimle pulled Skye behind her and threw up a magical ward of protection. She reached out and touched Senta's sword, concentrating to enchant it with a magic from the natural world. It began to grow green.

"Dallan," Gimle said, "Your sword!"

Dallan could barely take her eyes from the monstrosity towering over them. It was twelve feet high, not as large as the Marrow Shard they had faced years ago, but far more petrifying. The Marrow Shard was an enormous brute whereas this thing was the personification of evil.

"Dallan!" Gimle said sharply, and Dallan held out her sword, as did Rika. Gimle touched them, concentrated, and they began to glow with a soft green light. Skye just stood there numbly, then finally drew her own sword. Senta looked on with approval as Gimle enchanted Skye's sword as well. Senta was proud Skye had found her courage, but she would not let her out front.

"Stay behind me, and stay behind Gimle's ward," Senta said grimly, then turned back to the monster.

The Reaper Shard hovered about, its hunger voracious. The morsel it wanted, the delicacy it had stalked for weeks, was just feet away. The others were insignificant, although that one casting spells might taste good. But it was the small one in the middle the monster wanted.

It leaped toward them, its maw gaping, and Senta swung her sword at it. It cut through the creature, or would have had the creature not disappeared. It materialized a few feet away.

"It's behind us!" Rika screamed, and the band turned about to face the creature. Rika swung at the apparition and it again disappeared in a wisp of smoke, this time materializing right next to Dallan. Dallan thrust forward, but her sword thrust into the remains of blackened air as she lost her balance and Senta caught her.

The creature had some sort of primal intelligence, Senta thought, that much was clear. They could exhaust themselves swinging away at it while the thing phased in and out of their world.

"Pace yourselves," she cautioned, and they tightened their circle once more.

Gimle glanced down as Skye sheathed her sword. She thought at first Skye was giving up, but the girl removed the Tavinter bow from her back and an arrow from her quiver. She held it out to Gimle for an enchantment, and Gimle understood. She grasped the arrow by the shaft and concentrated her most powerful spell on the projectile. She had faith in Skye's ability, because she did not have much power left and she had just used most of it in that enchantment.

Skye notched the arrow in the bow and drew the string. The creature was still here, partially in this world, partially in the Underworld, she could feel it. The agitation that had been with her for weeks quieted, and she could hear her father Kolgrim whispering in her ear as he taught her to hunt.

"Relax your shoulders. Release your breath halfway."

And she did so. And then she heard her mother's voice, her beautiful, talented mother who somehow knew things that the other Tavinter did not. "Close your eyes Skye, for you have a gift the others do not. They know where the enemy is, but you know where the enemy will be."

Skye turned to her right and in a seemingly random move, released the arrow into empty space. But just as she released, the Reaper Shard materialized directly in her arrow's path and just as it fully formed, it was impaled by the enchanted missile. It screamed in agony and fury, writhed about in a frenzied mass of smoke, then dissipated into nothingness.

"You did it!" Dallan yelled joyfully, and Rika pounded her on the back. Skye looked ecstatic for a moment, then her expression fell.

"What's wrong?" Senta asked.

"There are more of them," Skye said quietly, dejectedly, and with complete resignation. It was the resignation in her voice that chilled Senta to the bone.

"How many more of them?" Senta asked. Gimle was exhausted and it wasn't likely they could defeat even one more, let alone more than one.

"A lot more," Skye said.

And no sooner were those words out of her mouth than the creatures began to spawn from the earth, rising up from the tiles one-by-one. Each screamed as it solidified into a corporeal form, and the noise was horrific.

They were surrounded by no less than twelve Reaper Shards that formed a circle about the small band of women. They gnashed their teeth and flitted about, each preparing to go in for the kill to get a piece of that morsel that had just revealed even more of its power.

"By the Divine," Halla whispered in horror from the balcony. She was about to watch all that she loved destroyed.

"They're after me," Skye said, somehow sensing their intent. She did not know why, but she knew the creatures had come for her. "You should leave me."

Rika looked over at her in exasperation. "Really, Skye? Do you think any of us are leaving you?"

Her words brought comfort to Skye, but they changed nothing. They could not survive this, and the only hope for the others was for her to draw the monsters away. That was her plan, anyway, until the first three Reaper Shards rose to their full, imposing heights, then snaked downward in a slamming movement that caused everyone to dive in different directions, separating them anyway. Senta swung at the one nearest her, as did Dallan and Rika, but it was to no avail as they were swinging at thin air.

Fortunately, Gimle landed near Skye and was able to throw up a protective ward in front of the girl as one of the Reaper Shards dove downward to gulp her whole. Skye stared up into the gaping maw, and the gullet of the beast went on forever. She rolled away, dashing to and fro to dodge the acidic tendrils lashing out at her. One caught her leg and it burned like fire, but she swung her sword and amputated the limb. Senta was fighting to get back to Skye but was easily thwarted by a single Reaper while all the others bedeviled Skye. Dallan and Rika were fighting a similar battle, and when Rika went down, Dallan had to redirect her attention to help her friend. Gimle was essentially unarmed and now that her power was exhausted, two Reapers turned to her and Skye watched in horror as she thought the mage was about to be eaten. But then she could not see Gimle because her view was blocked by the four Reaper Shards about to consume her. She held up her hands, hoping that her death would at least be quick as she stared up into the endless rows of teeth that led straight into the Underworld.

But then the Reaper was gone, disappearing into a whirlwind of flashing green blades that dispatched all four of the creatures before they knew they were being set upon. And the blades were devastatingly effective because they had been enchanted by one of the most powerful mages in all of Arianthem, a protégé of a legendary wizard and the daughter of a dragon, and even more so because they were wielded by the last Scinterian in all the world.

Raine whirled about and attacked the Reapers that had pinned Gimle. The creatures were so startled they barely reacted before being dispatched from the mortal realm with great violence. Gimle stared up at the beautiful woman whose blue-and-gold markings stood out on her forearms and the parts of her shoulders and back that were visible, and really, the Scinterian warrior seemed to be part demon herself. She was full of lighting and fury, turning on the other six of the Reapers and taunting them. Only one was so foolish as to attack and she met the ill-advised assault with a thrust that went straight through the creature's black heart, causing it to scream horrifically and disappear in a chaotic frenzy of smoke.

The other five milled about uncertainly, wavering in a hazy, indecisive manner. Raine did not hesitate.

"To my back!" she commanded, taking the opportunity to regroup, and Skye and the Ha'kan all moved in behind her. Rika felt a thrill, for they had gone from certain defeat and death to an almost certain victory within seconds. She would follow Raine through the gates of Hel itself.

Queen Halla could scarcely believe her eyes and did not even want to entertain hope. But the minute Astrid had pointed out the figure on horseback as it raced through the palace gates, that hope had flourished against all reason. And when the figure leaped from the horse right through the magical wall, untouched by the enchanted barrier, the hope burned brighter. And when Raine unleashed her wrath upon the monstrosities in a cloud of flashing green light, the hope turned to assurance.

The five Reaper Shards wavered, then disappeared. Raine did not lower her guard.

"Wait," she commanded, and her companions did so. No one moved, no one even breathed.

"There's something else here," Skye whispered. "Something worse."

"I know," Raine said quietly, and there was the same note of resignation in her voice that Senta had heard in Skye's earlier. And if that resignation had chilled Senta before, it filled her with utter dread now. Strangely, Raine stood upright and sheathed her swords. She removed the fine leather gloves that Elyara had crafted for her so she could wield enchanted weapons.

"These won't help me against this."

Directly in front of Raine, the air began to twist and turn in miniature vortexes. It formed into a yellowish, oily smoke that in turn began to form into an amalgam of limbs and body parts. The Ha'kan stared in horror at the creature. They had heard legend of the Membrane, the atrocity that seduced the living then absorbed their souls. Arms, legs, breasts, partial faces, sexual organs, all writhed about pleasuring and torturing one another. The creature appeared to be in a perpetual, painful orgasm as lips suckled and licked and chewed, fingers stroked and penetrated and thrust, and certain parts sodomized themselves while other lips cried out in climax and pain. It shifted, it throbbed, it pulsated; it was utterly disgusting, and they could not look away.

Raine felt very, very cold and as fearless as she was, she wanted to flee.

"Raine—?" Senta said.

"Whatever you do, Senta, don't touch it, don't any of you touch it." Raine said quietly. "And if it touches me, don't help me."

"Raine!" Senta said.

But Raine stood before the creature as it flowed toward her, sighing in delight. It settled upon her and Raine clenched her jaw to muffle a cry. Skye started toward her but Senta caught the girl before she could do anything foolish, and they both stared in horror as the Membrane stroked the arms, legs, and torso of the Scinterian warrior. It was like watching someone be sexually assaulted in front of them, and indeed the creature seemed intent on escalating to rape. The mouths of the creature moaned with pleasure as it flowed about over Raine's body, the fingers caressing, the lips feathering kisses, the tongues licking playfully down her legs and hovering so close to that which they desired.

And then, when it seemed it could get no worse, the amalgam shifted violently and stretched lengthwise so that it was now taller than Raine. A figure began to form in the mass of limbs, a woman's figure, a wickedly voluptuous figure, tall and perfect in form and feature. And the face began to materialize, and it was as stunningly beautiful as it was stunningly evil. And when the eyes opened, they were momentarily blood red with slit pupils like that of a snake, then transitioned to an emerald green that stared with an icy yet volcanic expression at the prize before her. The graceful limbs reached out and settled upon Raine's hips, pulling the unresisting woman toward her. And Raine tried to look away but the woman would not let her and cupped her chin in her hand and guided her back, pleased to see the violet in the eyes she had so effortlessly brought forth. And she lowered her head, touching her blood red lips to Raine's mouth and Raine made a weak effort to pull away, but the woman held her tight and kissed her more deeply, thrusting her tongue into that compliant mouth. And the woman pulled back just enough so that she could again look into those beautiful purple eyes.

"My love," she half-whispered, half-hissed.

"She is not your love," a low throaty voice behind the Membrane said as two hands with fingernails as strong as dragon's claws thrust through the center of the hideous creature. A stunning, silver-haired woman came through the Fade and materialized behind the monstrosity. She wore iridescent, fiery red armor the same color as a dragon's scales. The Membrane screamed, for it was sustaining actual damage whereas the woman inside of it just laughed for she was not really there and could not be hurt. The female apparition quickly dissolved back into the twisting mass of limbs, but the laughter could still be heard, echoing across the courtyard as Talan'alaith'illaria destroyed that manifestation of the Membrane. The overall creature could not be killed, but parts of it could definitely be neutered.

Raine collapsed into her lover's arms, and Weynild, although in human form, easily picked her up with the strength of her alternate form. Her lover was ice cold and she held her close to warm her.

"I knew you would come," Raine whispered, barely able to speak.

"My love," Weynild said, overcome. She wanted nothing more than to transform into her dragon form, put Raine upon her back and spirit her away to their mountain keep where she could protect her against all things. She had sensed from a distance what was transpiring and took a great risk in cutting through Nifelheim. But, as she turned her attention to the band of women staring at her, stunned, and the gathering crowd of dazed Ha'kan, she knew there was much to be done here and she could not leave.

"Is there someplace she can rest?" Weynild asked.

Senta shook herself from her frozen state. "Of course."

Queen Halla, accompanied by Astrid, Lifa, and Kara hurried to them and Halla overheard the request.

"Bring her to my forum, there's a guest room next to my chambers. You may stay as long as you wish. We're at your service."

Weynild carried Raine up the staircase, accompanied by the Queen and followed by her staff. Everyone stared at the silver-haired woman with the golden eyes, for she was a gorgeous, regal creature, older in appearance than her lover and fiercely elegant. And she carried Raine, who was not small, effortlessly.

Halla ushered them into a luxurious suite and Weynild moved to the great four poster bed where she sat Raine down gently. The others were torn between wanting to give the two their privacy and wanting to make sure that Raine was all right, and they hovered in the doorway. Weynild sat down next to Raine and pulled the cover over her because she was shaking with cold. Senta took it upon herself to come in and make a fire in the enormous fireplace, which she stoked until it was blazing. She stood back from the bed a respectful distance.

Raine drank in the sight of her lover. Weynild had been gone much longer than planned and she had desperately missed her. Weynild reached down and caressed her cheek.

"You should sleep," Weynild said, "the touch of the Membrane is not to be taken lightly, even by one such as you."

"It was not the Membrane's touch that drained me," Raine replied.

"I know," Weynild simply, then leaned down to kiss her. "I'm going to speak with them," she said, nodding toward the door, "then I'll be back to keep you warm."

Weynild walked out into the Queen's forum, and Halla settled into the circular seating area around the fire pit. Weynild blew out a breath toward the fire pit and it ignited into an inferno, a far more vigorous fire than that in the bedroom, perhaps stoked by the quiet rage of the dragon. The Ha'kan settled around their Queen, Senta protectively at her side, Dallan on the other. Skye sat down a little apart from the others, but Rika would have none of that and sat down right next to her, as did Gimle on her other side. Lifa, Astrid, and Kara settled in as well while Weynild stood, staring off in the distance with a thoughtful, seething look on her refined features.

"This is my fault," Skye said, "those creatures were after me."

Weynild laughed, a short, harsh sound, but the harshness was not directed at the girl. "No, little one, it's not your fault. It's my fault, and Isleif's, but not yours. We should have told you."

"Told me what?" Skye said, her hazel eyes filled with confusion.

Weynild appeared to be contemplating numerous things at once. "Those creatures were after you because you harbor enormous magical power."

"That can't be," Skye said, "I can barely cast a few spells."

"Your skill is untapped." Weynild glanced to Gimle. "As talented as the First Scholar is, you're going to require someone with very specific skills who can direct your ability." Weynild sighed. "She'll be here soon."

"How do you know this, this power?" Skye asked.

Weynild took a deep breath. So many secrets, and this would be just the first to come forth.

"Because Isleif is your great-grandfather."

Skye's mouth dropped open in astonishment and the heads of the Ha'kan jerked upward. All except those of the Queen and Astrid, and Dallan realized that her mother had known of Skye's heritage.

"Isleif tried to protect your mother," Weynild continued, brooding over her own words, "tried and failed. Those creatures came for her when he was not near, and she was overcome."

"No," Skye said, shaking her head, and Rika put her arm around her, hugging her. "My mother died from illness."

Weynild was quietly brutal in correcting her. "Your mother was poisoned when battling those creatures, poisoned to her very soul, and it was that illness that took her. Isleif was heartbroken when he lost her, and he held himself personally responsible. The magic had not manifested in your grandfather. Isleif prayed it would not manifest in Isolde."

"Why would he pray for such a thing?" Skye asked.

"Isleif has many powerful enemies, and he feared his offspring would be targets of revenge. His bloodline could be hidden within the Tavinter, but not if his children possessed his power."

"Why didn't he train my mother to use her power, so she could protect herself?"

"It's his greatest regret he did not," Weynild said, then was quiet for a moment. "He was filled with indecision, should he train Isolde openly? Or hope that her power would remain dormant? He chose the latter path."

"For many years it appeared he had made the right decision. He was able to protect the Tavinter and Isolde from a distance. Isolde became a great leader, and little of her power was evident. When she married your father, Kolgrim, Isleif was pleased beyond measure."

"Did my mother know any of this?" Skye asked. "Did she know Isleif was her grandfather?"

"No. Although Isleif told me he thought Isolde realized it on her death bed. She begged him to protect you."

Skye's jaw clenched and the muscle in her cheek went into spasm. It was all too much.

"And so Isleif prayed that the magic wouldn't manifest in you, but there were already signs. And he feared his power was waning, so he did two things." Weynild turned to the Queen. "When you approached Kolgrim with the proposal for an exchange, Kolgrim was against it. It was Isleif who convinced him that Skye would be safest with the Ha'kan for a few years, a mighty military power but a people with little penchant for magic. It pained him to deceive you through omission, but he felt he had little choice."

Halla carefully considered her words. "We would have taken Skye in, anyway."

Weynild allowed herself a slight smile. "I know."

Skye felt terrible. She had endangered her beloved friends, she had endangered the Ha'kan, and she had endangered Raine who kept having to rescue her.

"Is that why that sorceress Ingrid hates me?"

Weynild allowed herself another slight smile, although this one was not as pleasant. "I'm not sure 'hate' is the appropriate term. But yes, she's obsessed with you because she and Isleif were once lovers until he 'comforted' your great-grandmother in her grief, and your grandfather was born of that union. Her desire for revenge has taken a somewhat perverse turn with you, but then again she's a perverse individual."

"But this is still all my fault," Skye insisted, "everyone is in danger because of me. Even Raine."

"Don't underestimate Raine, there's very little that's a danger to my love." Weynild said with another slight smile. The smile then disappeared. "And what is most dangerous to her has nothing to do with you."

"That woman," Lifa murmured, "the one that formed inside that horrible creature."

Lifa had watched from the balcony adjacent to the Queen's terrace, horrified and mesmerized by that awful, beautiful woman who had materialized inside the writhing mass of limbs and set upon Raine like she owned her. Lifa may not have understood all the machinations involved, but she knew lust when she saw it. "She's the danger to Raine."

"Yes. But that was no woman," Weynild said calmly, her expression very dark. "It was a goddess."

This produced audible gasps about the room.

Kara thought furiously. She had stood next to Lifa on the balcony and been as horrified as she, but the woman's face had been familiar to her. She now recalled seeing a depiction of the gates of the Underworld in one of her ancient scrolls. That woman's image had been carved on the immense doors.

"That was Hel, wasn't it?" Kara said.

"Yes, that was Hel."

This pronouncement silenced the room completely. Hyr'rok'kin, Marrow Shards, even Reaper Shards were one thing, but the Goddess of the Underworld was another. And both Lifa and Astrid, attuned to the subtleties of their Ministry, discerned something elusive in Weynild's tone, something that suggested a deeper connection between the dragon and the Goddess.

"Hel was behind the Hyr'rok'kin invasion twenty years ago, and she's orchestrating the one that's beginning now." Weynild looked at Skye. "And so you must prepare. You must learn to use your magical abilities. Which brings me to the second thing that Isleif did. Although his power has waned, his mind has not. He has spent the last decade passing on his knowledge to a very powerful mage, your new mentor. She'll be here within a few days."

"And oh," Weynild said, as if it had almost slipped her mind, "she's my daughter."

"By the gods," Skye murmured, articulating everyone's surprise, "your daughter?"

"Yes," Weynild said, "she's half-human and therefore not a dragon, but her dragon's blood has made her immensely powerful."

Weynild turned to Senta. "And the Ha'kan must prepare for war, but it will be one unlike any they have ever fought. It will take Raine several weeks to recover, but she'll be at your service to help you prepare for the Hyr'rok'kin."

Senta nodded. "We'll begin as soon as she's ready."

Weynild turned at last to Queen Halla. "The Alfar will be here within a few weeks. I cannot stress enough the importance of an alliance, not just with them, but with the imperials as well. The empire will be sending a contingency, and that will be an opportunity for diplomacy. It's my guess that the grace and tact of the Queen of the Ha'kan will be crucial in this process."

Queen Halla nodded. "We'll use every resource at our disposal. And you and Raine will be staying here?" she asked hopefully.

"Yes," Weynild said, "indefinitely, if we're not imposing."

Halla could not hide her relief. "Our home is yours."

"Thank you for your hospitality." She addressed the group as a whole. "I know this is happening very quickly, and many things are hard to grasp. But I tell you this, everything that has happened was foreseen not just by me, but by the elven seer Y'arren and by Isleif as well. And as things continue to unfold, there will be great periods of darkness and sacrifice. But I promise you, I have seen to the end of this, and it will end in only one way."

Weynild looked about at the somber but determined group. "I'm going to go keep my love warm until she recovers."

Weynild was wrapped about Raine, who, once reunited with her dragon lover, fell into a deep, dreamless sleep. Weynild could not sleep, however, for her anger burned at the Goddess and she was tempted to fly into the heart of the Underworld and challenge Hel face to face. But she knew that such a rash response was what Hel wanted, and therefore she would not give her that satisfaction.

She startled herself awake, surprised that she had fallen asleep. Raine was no longer in bed with her but stood at the window, the blanket draped over her shoulders. Weynild rose and pulled on the Ha'kan robe that had been left for her. She rarely wore anything other than her armor which was actually a part of her, and the soft fabric felt strange against her skin. She walked to the window and put her hands about Raine, but Raine was stiff and tense in her embrace. Weynild looked over her shoulder, and the eyes that stared out at nothing were storm gray.

"Tell me what you're thinking," Weynild said.

Weynild thought at first Raine was not going to respond, but finally she did. Her tone was quiet, subdued, filled with self-recrimination.

"If Hel captures me, I won't be able to resist her."

"I know that," Weynild said.

"My mind and my heart will not be willing," Raine said, "but my body will betray me."

"You're Arlanian," Weynild said, "I expect nothing else."

Raine's jaw clenched. Her anger at her mother's people and their weakness burned.

"You've never experienced this before, have you?" Weynild asked.

"What?"

"Met someone stronger than you, someone you couldn't defeat or defend yourself from."

"Only you," Raine replied.

"That's different," Weynild said, "you're in love with me."

Raine was quiet for a while, then spoke again. "I think in a way I always despised the Arlanians," Raine said. "Wondering how they could allow themselves to be raped into extinction. And yet today I was as weak as any of them."

"I won't allow you to hate the part of you I so dearly love," Weynild said firmly. "If Hel takes you to her bed, then so be it. I will not condemn you for being what you are."

"It's not just that I'll be raped," Raine said with disgust, "it's that I'll yield and enjoy it."

"Then I suggest you learn to think more like the Ha'kan," Weynild said, "for they have the extraordinary ability to separate physical pleasure from love. Hel can force physical pleasure from you, but she can't take your love. That belongs to me."

Raine's eyes at last transitioned back to the violet color that normally looked upon Weynild. "You're so pragmatic about certain things," Raine said, relaxing in her lover's embrace.

"Well," Weynild said, her golden eyes gleaming, "the thought of you and Hel enrages me, but it's her I'll kill, not you."

Weynild sat down on the lounge which was large enough for Raine to sit in front of her. Raine removed the blanket from her shoulders so she could press her naked back against Weynild, then pulled the blanket over them both. Weynild was pleased that Raine's skin had warmed and now was only cool to the touch. She buried her face in Raine's hair and they were quiet for a while.

"So, you're still determined to follow through with this?" Raine asked.

"Have you changed your mind?" Weynild asked. "You know I won't force you."

Raine was silent for an extended period of time, thinking through every possibility.

"No," she said at last, "if this ends as you say it will, I'll endure anything."

She relaxed fully and pressed back against the softness of Weynild's breasts, feeling the tell-tale signs that her movement had aroused the dragon. Despite the dark events of the day, a trace of mischief crept into her voice.

"I know a way that you could warm me."

"Yes, and that way would delay your recovery by weeks," Weynild said dryly.

"I'm willing to take that chance," the dragon's lover said, and leaned back to kiss her love.

www.ingramcontent.com/pod-product-compliance
Lightning Source LLC
Chambersburg PA
CBHW071939170626
46813CB00005B/1790